MANDIE
AND THE
MIDNIGHT
JOURNEY

Mandie Mysteries

MANDIE
AND THE
MIDNIGHT
JOURNEY

Lois Gladys Leppard

BETHANY HOUSE PUBLISHERS
MINNEAPOLIS, MINNESOTA 55438
A Division of Bethany Fellowship, Inc.

Mandie and the Midnight Journey
Lois Gladys Leppard

Library of Congress Catalog Card Number 89-61622

ISBN 1-55661-084-X

Published by Bethany House Publishers
A Division of Bethany Fellowship, Inc.
6820 Auto Club Road, Minneapolis, Minnesota 55438

Printed in the United States of America

For My Dear Friend and Editor,

Carol A. Johnson,

With love and gratitude,

Without whom this book never would have been.

He that loveth his brother abideth in the light,
and there is none occasion of stumbling in him.
1 John 2:10

About the Author

LOIS GLADYS LEPPARD has been a Federal Civil Service employee in various countries around the world. She makes her home in Greenville, South Carolina.

The stories of her own mother's childhood are the basis for many of the incidents incorporated in this series.

Contents

Chapter 1 / Changes at Home

As the noisy train chugged to a stop in Franklin, North Carolina on a warm June day in 1901, Mandie picked up her small valise and eagerly scrambled out of her seat. The train let off a big puff of steam by the depot platform, and the passengers started to get off. Mandie hurried down the aisle ahead of Dr. Woodard.

"No need to rush," Dr. Woodard told the blond twelve-year-old girl. "I see Abraham out there. We'll have to wait until he gets your trunk and bags off the train."

Mandie stopped behind another passenger in the doorway. "I just wanted to get outside in the nice clean air after this sooty train ride," she replied. "Besides, I'm so happy that school's over for the summer, I can hardly wait to get home."

Dr. Woodard came up beside her. "I'm sure your mother and your Uncle John are looking forward to your coming home, too," he said.

The other passengers stepped down from the train, and Mandie quickly followed. She saw Abraham waiting at the end of the platform in her Uncle John's rig. She waved and ran to meet him, with Dr. Woodard following.

"Abraham!" she called out as she approached him. "I thought maybe Uncle John would meet us here at the depot."

"Mistuh John he be in Richmond on bidness," Abraham replied. He took her bag and put it in the rig. "I'se got to git yo' luggage, Missy. Be right back."

Dr. Woodard stopped by the rig. "Mandie, I have to get my buggy from the livery stable," he said. "Would you please tell your mother that I'll be along later? I have to see a patient or two, and then I'll see y'all."

"Of course, Dr. Woodard." Mandie smiled down at him. "Thank you for riding home from Asheville with me on the train."

"It was my pleasure, dear," he said, turning to leave. "And I look forward to visiting at your house tonight as well."

Mandie told him goodbye and watched as Abraham and the railroad baggage man hefted her heavy trunk onto the back of the rig. Then after piling several other valises on, Abraham climbed up beside Mandie, and they headed for her Uncle John's house, where she lived. Her mother, Elizabeth, had married Mandie's uncle after Mandie's father died.

As they rode down the main street of Franklin, Mandie looked over at the Negro man who worked for her uncle. "Is Snowball all right, Abraham?" she asked.

"Dat kitten he be fine and into ev'rything," Abraham replied. "When dat Injun man brung him from yo' grandma's he seemed like he proud to be home. Now dat noo baby, dat's 'nuther story. I don't believes dat noo baby like dis world. It cry and cry and—"

"Abraham . . ." Mandie quickly changed the subject. "Have you seen Polly Cornwallis next door? Is she home from school yet?"

"I believe she git home yistiddy," Abraham told her. "Anyhow she come over to see de noo baby yistiddy, and—"

"Abraham," Mandie interrupted impatiently, "I don't want to talk about that new baby."

"But Missy, dat baby be yo' mother's and yo' Uncle John's baby," the old man said.

"That's exactly why I don't want to discuss it," Mandie replied quickly. "Now let's talk about something else."

Abraham glanced back at her in alarm. Mandie was not usually so sharp-tongued.

Unable to think of anything to say in her misery, Mandie remained silent the rest of the way home. This new baby had already caused so much trouble and inconvenience for her, and now she was finally going to have to see it for the first time.

The baby would probably still be small and bothersome since it was only born a few weeks before. Mandie had already made up her mind to ignore the baby. She didn't want anything to do with it.

After all, it was only a half sister or half brother to her, or maybe it was a cousin since her Uncle John was its father. This was all so confusing!

What irritated her more was that her mother hadn't even let her know whether the baby was a boy or girl. And since Mandie refused to discuss it on the train with Dr. Woodard, he hadn't told her either—even though he had delivered the baby. So now she simply referred to the baby as "it."

Abraham pulled the rig to a halt in front of the white picket fence surrounding John Shaw's huge white house. Jumping down, he unlatched and opened the gate, then returned to the rig and drove it through.

As he stopped the vehicle again, Mandie quickly stepped down into the green grass. "Go ahead, Abraham," she said. "I'll latch it."

Abraham nodded and drove on into the backyard. Mandie fastened the gate and hurried up the walkway to the long front porch.

As soon as she opened the screen door, she found Snowball at her feet, meowing at her. Mandie scooped him up in her arms and rubbed her face against his. The white kitten closed his eyes and purred loudly.

Suddenly, Mandie heard the piercing wail of a baby screaming. It sounded as if it was coming from somewhere upstairs. Mandie froze. *What on earth is wrong with that baby, howling like that?* she thought.

Just then Aunt Lou, the old Negro housekeeper, hurried into the hallway. When she saw Mandie standing there, she ran over and gave her a big hug. "I sho' be glad to see you home, my chile," the huge old woman told her. Aunt Lou patted Mandie's blond head.

"Oh, Aunt Lou, I'm glad to see you, too," Mandie said as the baby's cries grew louder. "But what is going on with all that screaming?"

"Dat baby jes' don't like bein' bawn in dis world," the old woman replied. "It cry and it cry all de time. Yo' po' ma she cain't sleep or eat or nuthin', it cry so."

"Humph!" Mandie grunted, clutching Snowball tighter as she turned away. "I'm going to my room, Aunt Lou."

"No, no, no, my chile," the old housekeeper scolded.

"You gwine right upstairs and see yo' ma. Let huh know you's home."

"I'm tired, Aunt Lou," Mandie protested.

"Dat don't make no never mind," Aunt Lou said. "Yo' ma she be tired, too, but she waitin' fo' you to come home. Now git up dem steps." The old woman gave her a little shove.

Mandie sighed. Not knowing what else to do, she started upstairs, petting Snowball as she went. Then she stopped. "Aunt Lou, you come with me," she pleaded. "Please?"

"Well, all right," the old woman agreed, trudging up the stairs behind the girl.

The screaming grew louder as they walked along the hallway upstairs, and Snowball climbed up on Mandie's shoulder. Mandie halted at the open door of her mother's sitting room.

Elizabeth sat in a rocking chair, trying to quiet the baby's screams. Back and forth she rocked, talking quietly into the baby's ear.

Aunt Lou nudged Mandie forward, but the girl wouldn't budge. The noise was deafening. *I didn't realize that such a little thing could make such a big noise,* she thought. Putting her hands over her ears, she frowned. Snowball clutched the shoulder of her dress.

Elizabeth turned and saw Mandie standing in the doorway. She looked pale and worn out, but she smiled. "Welcome home, dear," she said above the howling. Put that cat down out there and come see the baby."

Mandie couldn't move. "I will later when all that screaming stops," she hollered over the noise.

Elizabeth laughed weakly. "It may never stop," she said.

"Then I may never come to see it," Mandie replied curtly.

Aunt Lou gasped and poked Mandie from behind.

Elizabeth looked directly at Mandie. "Oh, but you will, Amanda," she said loudly. "You're excused for now, but you *will* see the baby later."

Full of resentment, Mandie turned and raced back down the hallway and around the corner to her room. She pushed the door open and found her trunk and bags sitting in the middle of the floor. Closing the door, she flopped down on the blue silk bedspread with the kitten in her arms and began talking to him. She could still hear the baby screaming in the distance.

"What are we going to do, Snowball?" she asked the kitten. "We can't stand all that screaming and carrying on. That baby is a brat. That's what it is—a brat!" She wiped her teary eyes.

Snowball meowed and purred.

Just then the door opened and Liza, the Negro maid, danced into the room.

Mandie sat up quickly.

Liza grinned. "I sho' is glad to see you, Missy 'Manda," she said. "Dat howlin' baby's 'bout to drive us all batty, sho' 'nuff."

Mandie jumped up to embrace her friend. "I'm glad to be home, Liza. But I didn't expect all that noise."

"You ain't heerd de half of it, Missy," Liza told her. "It go on all day and all night it do. And we'se rubbed our hands raw washin' dem baby diapers. De clothesline it stay full of wavin' white diapers."

Mandie sat in a nearby chair and looked up at the maid. "Does that baby really cry all the time?"

Liza nodded. "Jes' about."

"Is it sick or what?"

"Dat doctuh man say he cain't find nuthin' wrong," Liza replied, walking over to Mandie's trunk. She tried to open it.

"It's locked," Mandie said.

"You got de key, Missy?" Liza asked. "Aunt Lou say I got to git dis heah trunk unpacked befo' suppertime."

Mandie reached inside the small valise she had carried on the train and pulled out the key. "I'll help so we can talk." She opened the trunk and threw back the lid.

Liza was not much older than Mandie and the two were good friends. The Negro girl always seemed to know everything that was going on around the Shaw house. As they shook out dresses from the trunk and hung them in the huge wardrobe, Liza brought Mandie up to date.

"Yo' Uncle John he done gone to Richmond on bidness, he *say*," Liza told her. "I say he go to git 'way from de screamin'."

Mandie looked at her and laughed. "But Liza, I don't think Uncle John would go all the way to Richmond to get away from the noise. He could just go downtown for awhile."

Liza put Mandie's bonnets on the top shelf of the wardrobe. "But he cain't stay long downtown," she said. "Anyhow, I thinks yo' ma, she oughtta go some place, too. Miz 'Lizbeth look plumb wore out."

"That's *their* problem!" Mandie snapped. She leaned into the trunk to retrieve another dress. "They wanted the baby, so now they have to put up with it."

Liza stopped putting the clothes away, propped her hands on her hips, and frowned at Mandie. "Dat baby be yo' kin, too," she scolded.

Mandie straightened up. "But I didn't ask for a baby," she argued. "It wasn't my idea. They can . . . they can . . . give it away, for all I care!"

Liza's eyes grew wide. "Missy!"

Mandie blew out her breath. "Well, at least I won't have to put up with that baby for the whole month of July."

"And where is you gwine to be gone to?" Liza questioned.

"Didn't you know, Liza?" Mandie's blue eyes sparkled with excitement. "I'm going to Europe with my grandmother and my friend back at school, Celia Hamilton."

"Dat's de first I'se heerd of it," Liza said. "Europe? Where dat be, Missy?"

"Europe is all the way across the ocean," Mandie explained. "We're going to sail on one of those huge passenger ships like I saw when we were in Charleston, South Carolina, last year."

Liza shook her head slowly. "What fo' you wants to be traipsin' all over de place?" she persisted. "You goes to dat Washington town to see dat President man clear out o' dis part o' de country, and now you says you gwine ride out on all dat water." Liza threw her hands up in the air. "Lawsy mercy, Missy, s'pose dat ship git a hole in it. You cain't swim. Whatcha gwine do den?"

"Liza, my grandmother and I have already discussed all this," Mandie told her. "The ship will have a lot of small boats on it, and if the big ship starts to leak or sink, then they put all the little boats in the water. And all the passengers get into the boats and wait for another big ship to pick them up. That's all there is to it," Mandie explained. She started hanging up her dresses again.

"Dat ain't all dere is to it," Liza contradicted her,

watching Mandie do the work. "S'pose no big ships find out you ridin' 'round in dem li'l boats? You cain't stay dere forever. You gotta eat sometime."

"Liza, all the big ships can send messages to other boats. Our ship would let another one know that we needed help," Mandie replied.

Liza grunted. "Humph! Wouldn't ketch me on dem big ships or dem li'l boats, neither. I cain't swim."

"I can't either, but I wouldn't be afraid—I don't think," Mandie said.

Liza shook out the last dress from the trunk, and the girls quickly unpacked the rest of Mandie's bags. Then when Liza had to go downstairs to set the table for supper, Mandie decided to take a bath.

Flipping through the dresses hanging in her wardrobe, she picked a white voile dress with tiny blue embroidered flowers and laid it out on her bed. In this unusually warm June weather, the voile dress would be cool.

The whole time Mandie was bathing, she heard the baby screaming down the hall. Mandie dreaded having to face her mother at the supper table.

The more she thought about it, the more she wished she didn't have a vacation from school. She would rather be back there with Celia than have to listen to this howling all day long.

As Mandie got dressed, she surveyed herself in the long mirror in her room. She was sure that even Miss Prudence back at school would be proud of her. Mandie had the ladylike look that the headmistress and Miss Hope had tried so hard to teach their students.

As she stared into the mirror, Mandie realized that she was getting taller. After all, she would be thirteen years old in a few days.

Above the sound of the baby's crying, a quick knock on the door made Mandie jump. Liza entered the room abruptly. "Miz 'Lizbeth, she say tell you she cain't eat supper at de table tonight 'cause de baby keep cryin'," Liza explained.

"You mean I have to eat supper alone?" Mandie whined.

"Mistuh Bond, he be back. He be heah fo' supper tonight," Liza told her. "I got to go take a tray to yo' ma now." She danced out of the room.

Mandie sighed. That baby kept on interfering with everything. Mandie plopped down in a chair and put her hands over her ears as the little one's yelling continued. She waited until the little ceramic clock on her mantelpiece struck six. Then she went downstairs.

Jason Bond stood waiting in the hallway for her. "Welcome home," the old caretaker said, going ahead to push open the door to the dining room.

Mandie smiled. "Thank you, Mr. Jason," she returned.

Inside the dining room, the table before them was loaded with food. Mandie noticed that a place had been set for her mother. As she and Mr. Bond sat down, Mandie looked up at Liza nearby. "Is Mother coming down, after all?" she asked.

"No, Missy, I jes' left dem dishes there 'cause I ain't had time to move 'em," the maid replied, picking up the china. "Here, I'll jes' put 'em on de side heah. Maybe dat doctuh man come in time to eat."

Mandie shook out the linen napkin by her place and laid it in her lap. "When I left Dr. Woodard at the depot, he said he'd be here later," she told Liza, "so maybe he will arrive in time for the meal."

After giving thanks for their food, Mr. Bond asked about her upcoming journey overseas. Mandie noticed he carefully avoided mentioning the new baby.

"You're a brave little lady to get on one of those big ships and sail all the way across the ocean," the caretaker said, helping himself to the fried chicken.

Mandie spooned green beans onto her plate. "Have you ever been to Europe, Mr. Jason?" she asked.

"Goodness, no," Mr. Bond replied. "I'm satisfied staying right here where I belong. Ain't got no hankering to cross all that water."

"I'm anxious to go," Mandie said excitedly. "I think I'll really enjoy it. You know my grandmother has been to Europe several times, and she has told me so much about everything over there that I just can't wait to see it!" Mandie took a bite of her chicken.

The caretaker grinned. "Well, you're young and should enjoy it," he said. "Me, I'm too old for that kind of a lark."

Mandie noticed that she could still hear the baby crying, even with the doors closed. "Mr. Jason, do you think there's something wrong with that baby?" she ventured.

Jason Bond swallowed a bite of food and smiled at her. "Dr. Woodard says the baby's normal—no health problems he can see," the man replied. "Maybe that poor child just needs to get used to us all."

At that moment, Liza came in from the hall, and Mandie heard another piercing wail from the baby. "Well, I sure wish it'd hurry up," she said, drumming her fingers on the table. "That crying is one big reason why I'll be glad to get away from here for a whole month." She took a drink of her iced tea.

Mr. Bond buttered a biscuit and took a bite. "Your mother is not very experienced at these things, you know," he said. "So if I were you, I'd kinda be patient."

"I know she doesn't have much experience," Mandie said, laying down her fork. "My Grandmother told my mother I was dead and gave me to my father. Then she told him never to come back."

"Now, now, Missy," the caretaker protested. "I know all about that. But it was all your grandmother's doing. She was the one who told your father that your mother didn't want you and never wanted to see him again." Mr. Bond sipped his coffee. "Don't blame your mother for that."

Mandie sat silently for a minute. "Well, if I had been in my mother's place," she said, "I would have demanded proof that my baby had died."

"You know your grandmother, Missy. She can be stern and bossy," Jason Bond replied.

Mandie sighed deeply. "Well, anyhow, I don't think Mother loves me as much as I love her," she said.

Liza opened the door and entered with fresh, hot biscuits. "De doctuh man be heah," she announced. "He be comin' right in to eat, he say."

As Liza danced out of the room, Dr. Woodard came in, sat down at the table. "Sorry I'm late for supper," he said, looking around the table. "Where's your mother, Amanda?"

Mandie took a deep breath. "Can't you hear that screaming going on? She's upstairs with that crying baby."

"I told her there's no reason for her to hold the baby every minute," Dr. Woodard said, helping himself to the beans. "Someone else ought to stay with it so she can at least come down and eat."

"I agree, Dr. Woodard," Mandie said. "But my mother is so wrapped up in the baby that she can't leave it long enough to join us for supper."

A look of concern flitted across the doctor's face. "Have you seen the baby, Amanda?"

"I've seen it, and all it was doing was screaming its head off while my mother held it," Mandie answered.

"Well, things should improve soon because there is nothing physically wrong with the baby that I can see," the doctor said. "In fact, your mother may have spoiled that child with all that holding and rocking all the time."

"You're probably right," Mandie agreed.

Liza danced into the dining room again. "Thought you might want to know, Missy. Miz 'Lizbeth done et her supper whut I took her, and she say fo' me to come right back and stay wid dat baby so she kin come down to de parlor for a while." Without waiting for a reply Liza slipped back into the kitchen.

Dr. Woodard and Mandie looked at each other.

"That's a good sign," the doctor said. "I'll hurry so we can join her in the parlor."

Mandie dreaded facing her mother, but she knew she had to. She felt guilty about the way she had reacted to her mother's request to come see the baby. At least her mother wouldn't have that crying infant with her in the parlor.

Chapter 2 / Cry, Cry, Cry!

Mandie and Dr. Woodard were already seated in the parlor when Elizabeth came downstairs. Dr. Woodard stood as she entered the room. The pretty blond woman was neatly dressed, as usual, but she looked tired and weak.

Mandie looked at her in alarm, then ran to embrace her. "I love you, Mother," she said.

"And I love you, darling. Let's sit down over here." Elizabeth indicated a settee by the window opposite where Dr. Woodard had been sitting. "And I thank you, Dr. Woodard, for escorting Amanda home from school."

Dr. Woodard nodded. "I was glad to do so, Elizabeth. It was no inconvenience at all," he said. "Now if you'll excuse me for a few minutes, I think I'll speak to Mr. Bond about something."

Elizabeth smiled. "Of course, Dr. Woodard, but do come on back," she urged. "I'm anxious to hear about your family."

As the doctor left the room, Elizabeth gently pulled Mandie down beside her on the settee. "I'm glad you're home, dear," she said. "We've been waiting for you to come home and name the baby."

Mandie frowned, nervously twisting her hands together in her lap. "I . . . I wouldn't know what to name a baby," she said haltingly. "You name it."

"The baby is not an *it,* Amanda. He's a boy. You have a little brother."

Well, at least that little mystery is solved, she thought. *And I'm still the only daughter, anyway.*

"Your Uncle John and I thought you might like to name him," Elizabeth went on. "And John suggested naming him James after your father, dear."

Mandie sprang up from the settee. "No!" she protested. "No one is to have my father's name. He's not my father's son!"

Elizabeth looked at her in alarm. "But dear, we all loved your father so much that—"

"Nobody loved my father as much as I did," Mandie insisted. She quickly turned away. "I need a drink of water," she said in a shaky voice, running from the room.

When Mandie entered the kitchen, no one was there. She reached for a glass in the cupboard and then burst into tears. *Nobody understands how I feel,* she thought. *Nobody cares about me. All they care about is that squalling baby!*

Aunt Lou opened the door and stopped in the doorway. She walked over and put her strong arms around the girl's shoulders. "What fo' you be cryin', my chile?" she asked.

Mandie buried her face against Aunt Lou's ample bosom and cried uncontrollably.

Aunt Lou patted the girl's blond head. "Now you listen

to me," she said. "You jes' got to quit dis heah cryin'. You're gwine ruin dem pretty blue eyes. 'Sides, cryin' ain't gwine change nuthin'. Dat baby done got bawn, and he be heah to stay. So you might as well git used to it. Now hush up dat cryin', dis heah instant!"

Mandie caught her breath and looked up into the old Negro woman's stern face. She had never seen Aunt Lou look so cross. She tried to control the sobs as Aunt Lou lifted the skirt of her big white apron and dried the girl's tears.

"I be surprised at you actin' like dis," the housekeeper scolded. "Yo' po' ma ain't none too well, and she doin' huh best to straighten out dat cryin' baby. You oughta be ashamed of yo'self."

Mandie looked up into the woman's black face. "Is my mother sick, Aunt Lou?" she asked anxiously.

"Not exactly whut you calls sick 'cept she done wore out wid dat baby cryin' all day and all night," the housekeeper explained. "She cain't git no rest. She need yo' help."

"My help?" Mandie frowned. "I don't know anything about babies. I've never even been around one before."

"Well, you'se 'round one now, and it be time fo' you to learn," Aunt Lou told her. "Den when you gits grown and married, you'll know how to tend to yo' own babies."

"I may get grown. I can't stop that," Mandie said. "But I may *never* get married, not if it means having crying babies like that one."

Aunt Lou smiled. "We'll see, my chile, when dat time comes. Now you wash dat face and march right back in dat parlor. Right now." She handed Mandie a towel from a nearby rack.

Mandie meekly turned and splattered water onto her face from the faucet in the sink. Then she dried off with the towel.

As she left the kitchen, Aunt Lou followed her to be sure she went back into the parlor. Mandie knew the old woman was standing in the hallway where Elizabeth couldn't see her. Aunt Lou was going to make sure that Mandie behaved.

Dr. Woodard had also returned to the parlor, and he and Elizabeth were talking, so Mandie silently slumped into a chair nearby.

"I was hoping you could stay until John gets back," Elizabeth told the doctor. "He'll be sorry he missed you."

"I have to leave tomorrow, unfortunately," the doctor replied. "But I'll be back this way soon." Turning to look at Mandie, he added, "I'll probably bring that son of mine with me next trip."

Mandie sat up. "Oh, please do, Dr. Woodard," she said. "I have lots of things to tell Joe about what's been going on at school and all."

Dr. Woodard smiled. "And I'm sure Joe will bring you up to date on happenings back at Charley Gap," he answered.

Elizabeth looked over at her daughter. "You and I have lots of things to talk about, too, Amanda," she said. "I want to hear all about your visit with President McKinley as soon as we have time to talk awhile without the baby interrupting."

There it was again! The baby was always getting in the way. Mandie took a deep breath to control her anger. She remained silent, afraid her voice would betray her feelings.

Dr. Woodard tried to break the tension. "Joe told us y'all had quite an adventure there in the White House."

Mandie brightened. "We did," she agreed. "President and Mrs. McKinley are both such nice people. And they never did find out about the mystery we solved."

Suddenly Aunt Lou stepped out of the shadows in the hallway, where she'd been keeping an eye on Mandie. She cleared her throat noisily. "Miz 'Lizbeth," she spoke up, "would you and de doctuh be carin' fo' some coffee maybe?"

Elizabeth looked up, surprised. "Why, Aunt Lou, that would be wonderful. Thank you."

Aunt Lou grinned broadly and beckoned to Mandie. "You come he'p me, my chile. We git dis coffee fixed in no time."

Relieved to get out of the room, Mandie hurried after Aunt Lou. But once they were inside the kitchen, the old housekeeper scolded her again.

"Now you listen heah, and listen good, my chile," the big Negro woman began, bending to look directly into Mandie's blue eyes. "You quit dat cold attitude toward yo' ma'. And I means it."

Mandie was beginning to wish she had stayed in the parlor.

"Yo' ma loves you, and I knows you loves her, so jus' cut out all dat silent, unfrien'ly way you be actin'. What be de mattuh wid you? Jealousy don't never do nuthin' but cause trouble. It have a way of eatin' a person up inside and messin' up his whole life. And you be headin' down dat troublesome lane, de way you'se doin'."

Mandie silently stared back at the dark eyes focused on her. She clasped her hands together behind her and stood on one side of her right foot.

"I'm tellin' you," Aunt Lou continued as she took the dishes down from the cupboard, "dat baby ain't gwine go 'way."

"I know that," Mandie admitted.

Aunt Lou put the dishes on a tray and went to the big iron cookstove where the coffeepot waited, steaming hot.

The old housekeeper filled a china pot with coffee. "Den why don't you be actin' like you knows it?" she growled.

"Aunt Lou, did you want me to come with you to get the coffee just so you could fuss at me?" Mandie sulked.

"Dat's 'zackly right," the old woman said, her eyes twinkling. "I been standin' there in de hallway listenin', and what I hears don't set good on my old ears." As she finished arranging some cookies on the tray, she turned to Mandie. "Just you wait till yo' Uncle John git home. He'll straighten you out. You'll see."

Mandie followed as the old woman carried the tray out of the kitchen. "There's nothing to straighten out, Aunt Lou," she insisted.

"You'll be seein'. Dis be *his* brand new baby. You jes' his niece. Remember dat," the old woman said as they walked toward the parlor.

Mandie tugged at the housekeeper's sleeve. They both stopped in the hallway. "You mean, Uncle John loves the baby more than he loves me?" she asked.

"Now, I didn't say dat, my chile," Aunt Lou said quickly. "What I means is dat he be proud of dat baby, and he gwine want you to be proud of it, too. You's gwine hurt his feelin's if you don't watch out."

Aunt Lou walked on down the hall as she continued.

"Dat man been good to you," she reminded Mandie. "You come heah wid no place to call home and he give you a home. You gotta quit dis selfish way you been actin'. De good Lawd say we's to love one 'nuther. Now git on in de parlor and behave yo'self."

Mandie said nothing. She was tired of everyone telling her how she was supposed to feel. She couldn't stand that baby. Nobody was going to make her love it.

Mandie didn't want her mother angry with her. She just wanted some time with her without any talk about the baby. But she said nothing and silently followed Aunt Lou back into the parlor. All the while she could hear that baby's muffled cries from upstairs.

As Aunt Lou set the tray in front of Elizabeth, Mandie sat down beside her mother.

Dr. Woodard whiffed the coffee aroma. "That smells like a right good pot of coffee, Aunt Lou," he said.

The old Negro smiled. "It be dat, it sho' is," she replied as she left the room.

Mandie thought things over quickly and decided to try to smooth over the tension between her and her mother. "It does smell delicious," she said, trying to smile, "and look at all those little cookies Aunt Lou put on the tray."

"Help yourself to those, dear," Elizabeth said. "I'd rather you didn't drink coffee at night, though."

"Thanks, Mother. I'll just take a couple of these." Mandie took a napkin off the tray and picked up two cookies. "I don't want any coffee anyway. But I'm worried about you. Everybody says you don't get much sleep because of the baby crying. Maybe you'd sleep better if you didn't drink coffee at night."

Elizabeth smiled as she poured some of the steamy black liquid for herself and the doctor. "Amanda, dear, I appreciate your concern, but you know this good coffee sort of peps up us older folks when we're tired."

Dr. Woodard tilted his head, listening. "Why, I do believe Liza has got that baby quiet," he said. "I don't hear him crying, do you?"

Elizabeth sipped the coffee from her cup. "She's probably rocking him and singing to him." She laughed. "Liza loves to sing to that baby." She set her cup down and turned to Mandie. "Why don't we go see how she got him quiet," she suggested. "You haven't really seen him yet, dear."

In spite of her good intentions, Mandie put her mother off. "I will tomorrow, Mother. I promise I'll go see him tomorrow."

Dr. Woodard nonchalantly sipped his coffee. "You know, he may be asleep, and you certainly don't want to wake him," he said.

Elizabeth picked up her coffee cup again. "You're right, Dr. Woodard." She smiled at Mandie. "We'll wait until tomorrow for your visit, dear."

"Thanks, Mother," Mandie said with a sigh of relief.

Elizabeth soon sent Mandie upstairs to go to bed. "You've had a long journey today," she said. "I want you to get a good night's rest now."

Mandie kissed her mother, then turned to the doctor. "Good night, Dr. Woodard," she said. "I'll see you at breakfast."

As she hurried up the steps, Snowball came running down the long hallway and followed her up to her room. He always seemed to know when it was eating or sleeping time.

Just as Mandie got to the top of the stairs, the baby started screaming again. Snatching up Snowball, Mandie raced down the hallway to her room and slammed the door. When she walked over to sit by the window, the cries seemed to drift in from outside.

The baby's probably by the open window in Mother's sitting room, she decided. It was too warm to close the window. Nervous and frustrated, Mandie walked around her room with her hands over her ears. Snowball followed his mistress from one side of the room to the other.

Suddenly Mandie stopped and picked up her kitten. "Come on, Snowball. Let's go outside away from that screaming."

She quietly crept down the hallway to the corner where it turned by the servants' stairs. Knowing her mother would hear the screaming and come up, Mandie slipped down the steps in the corner.

Arriving downstairs in a back hallway, Mandie softly opened the side door and hurried out into the yard. She rubbed her hand over her kitten's soft fur. "Let's go to the summerhouse," Mandie whispered.

Holding Snowball tightly, Mandie raced across the lawn in the shadow of the trees and made it to the summerhouse without anyone seeing her. She sat on one of the benches that encircled the inside of the structure and held Snowball in her lap. "You can't get down, Snowball. You'll run away. And if I have to go chasing after you, someone will see me in the moonlight."

Snowball finally quit squirming and curled up in Mandie's lap. Mandie leaned her head back to look at the moon and stars through the latticework of the summerhouse. *The moon's full tonight,* she thought.

Mandie heard a soft, familiar birdlike whistle. She jumped up and looked around. "Uncle Ned!" she cried as he came toward her in the shadows. "How did you know I was out here?" As her old Indian friend sat down, she dropped onto the bench beside him.

"I know Papoose come home today," the old Indian said, smiling at her. "And I see Papoose walk here when I go to door in house."

"Did you talk to my mother?"

"I see Papoose, so I not knock on door of house. I come here," Uncle Ned explained. "Why Papoose come here in dark?"

"That new baby just cries and cries," Mandie complained. "Even in my room with the door shut I could still hear him screaming."

"New papoose stop crying soon," Uncle Ned assured her.

"I sure hope so," Mandie said. Then she looked up into the old Indian's tanned, wrinkled face. "Do you want to go inside the house, Uncle Ned? My mother and Dr. Woodard are drinking coffee in the parlor."

"No, Papoose," he said. "I come see Papoose. Come see how Papoose like new papoose."

"You came all the way here just to ask how I like the new baby?" Mandie questioned.

"No. I visit friends up mountain over there. This on way," Uncle Ned said. "How Papoose like new brother?"

"He's not my brother," Mandie replied quickly. "Not my whole brother, that is. He's only my half brother."

Snowball jumped down to chase a lightning bug nearby.

Mandie watched the kitten for a moment. "He's really my cousin, too," she said. "Oh, it's all so confusing and aggravating. That baby interferes with everything. I can't even stay in the house because he cries so loud. I'll be glad to go to Europe with my grandmother in July. I wish I could stay with her all summer."

"Remember, Papoose, Big Book say must love brother. Papoose love mother. Papoose love Uncle John," the old Indian tried to explain. "Papoose must love everybody."

"I do love them, Uncle Ned," Mandie replied thoughtfully. "It's just that everybody keeps fussing at me about that baby, trying to tell me how to act and everything. And I don't like it."

"All know Papoose unhappy," Uncle Ned replied. "Want to help."

"Well, I wish they'd just quit bossing me," Mandie said curtly.

"Papoose . . ." Uncle Ned sounded disappointed in her. "Please try be happy about new papoose, please?" He took her small white hand in his old wrinkled one.

Mandie gazed up into his deep black eyes. She knew he loved her. Before her father died, he had promised to watch over her, and he had never let Mandie down. He was always there, helping her do what was right.

She smiled. "I promise, Uncle Ned," she said, then quickly added, "but it probably won't do any good."

"Keep promise, Papoose," he insisted.

"All right," she said. "I promise to keep my promise just for you, Uncle Ned."

The old Indian stood. "Must go now. See Papoose again soon."

"Good night, Uncle Ned." Mandie picked up Snowball. "I guess I'd better go back inside the house now."

Uncle Ned stood watching until Mandie was safely in the house. Then as she watched through the glass in the door, she saw him wave and disappear in the shadows.

Mandie crept up the stairs. The house was dark and quiet. Maybe the baby had gone to sleep.

But just as she entered her room and quietly closed the door, the screaming began again. This time it was fainter, though. Her mother must have closed all the windows and doors.

Mandie got undressed and slipped into bed with Snowball at her feet. But she lay awake long into the night as the baby cried on and on. It was too warm to put her head under the covers. She tried holding her hands over her ears, but her arms got tired.

She fluffed up the pillow and tried to bury her ears in it, but that didn't work, either. And every time Mandie moved, Snowball had to change his position on the bed to keep from getting squashed.

Mandie tossed and turned all night, remembering her promise to Uncle Ned. But how could she possibly be happy with that crying baby? Something had to be done about that.

Chapter 3 / Plans for Midnight

The next morning Elizabeth gently shook her daughter awake. "You're late for breakfast, dear," she said, sitting on the edge of the bed.

Mandie opened her still-sleepy eyes and sat up. It seemed as though she had just dozed off. Turning to sit beside her mother, Mandie reached up and put her arms around her. "Good morning, Mother," she said, laying her head on Elizabeth's shoulder.

Her mother smoothed back the long, tumbled blond hair. "Good morning, dear," she said. "You need to hurry to get downstairs for breakfast. Dr. Woodard will be leaving after we eat, you know."

Mandie stood up and stretched. "I'll be ready in a jiffy, Mother."

Elizabeth walked toward the door and opened it. "As soon as we finish breakfast, I'll take you to see your new brother. He seems to be in a quieter mood this morning. So please hurry, dear," she said, closing the door behind her.

As Mandie reached for a dress to put on, she remembered why she was so sleepy. *That baby cried all night, and now I suppose he's taking a little nap so he can holler all day,* she thought. *I hope he won't be screaming his head off when Mother takes me to see him later.*

Mandie dressed quickly and joined her mother, Dr. Woodard and Mr. Bond at the breakfast table. After the blessing was said, they began eating the huge breakfast Aunt Lou served. All the while Mandie kept her ears open, listening for the baby's cry any minute. But he never made a sound.

Dr. Woodard studied Mandie from across the table. "You look deep in thought, Amanda," he said.

Mandie took a deep breath and said the first thing that came into her mind. "I was just wishing that I could go home with you, Dr. Woodard, and visit awhile," she said quickly.

Dr. Woodard looked at Mandie's mother.

Elizabeth laid her fork down on her plate. "Why, you've just come home, dear. I couldn't let you go away so soon. Maybe later, that is, if Mrs. Woodard wouldn't mind." She sipped her coffee.

"Now, Elizabeth," Dr. Woodard said quickly, "you know my wife would be tickled pink to have Amanda visit us." Turning to Mandie, who hadn't said a word, he added, "Maybe when you come back from your trip to Europe you could come over for a few days."

Mandie's fork clattered to her plate in her excitement. "Could I, Mother? Please?" she asked.

Elizabeth sighed. "Of course you may, dear. It's just that I'm jealous of you and want you with me every minute possible."

Funny she should use that word, Mandie thought.

"But you have the baby now, Mother," she said, realizing that she was just trying to get away from him.

Elizabeth set her coffee cup on the table. "We'll see," she promised.

When they had all finished eating, Elizabeth turned to her daughter as Dr. Woodward stood up to take leave. "Now I don't want to rush you, Amanda, but I think we ought to go see your little brother before he begins one of those crying spells."

"Yes, Mother," Mandie agreed reluctantly.

Mr. Bond had been silent throughout the meal and now he quickly left, saying that he would see to Dr. Woodard's horse and buggy. "I thank you for everything, Elizabeth," the doctor said. "I have to be getting on my way now."

Mandie stood up to walk to the door with him. "Dr. Woodard," she said, "please tell Joe I hope he gets to come visit us before I go off to Europe in July."

"I certainly will, young lady," the doctor promised.

Elizabeth walked down the hall with them. At the door, she smiled at the old country doctor. "I hope we'll see you again soon, Dr. Woodard," she said, bidding him goodbye.

Dr. Woodard waved as he hurried down the long walkway to his horse and buggy, which Mr. Bond had waiting at the hitching post.

Elizabeth turned to Mandie. "Now, dear. Let's go see what your little brother is doing." She smiled and put an arm around Mandie's shoulder as they walked up the stairs.

When they entered Elizabeth's sitting room, they found Liza sitting by the cradle, gently rocking it with her foot.

As soon as Liza saw them, she stood up. "He been good, Miz 'Lizbeth," the Negro maid told her. "He ain't made a sound, not one."

Elizabeth smiled and Mandie thought she saw a look of relief in her mother's eyes. "Thank you for staying with him, Liza," she said. "Now you can go back downstairs and do whatever Aunt Lou has planned for you."

Liza flashed Mandie a quick grin, then left the room, closing the door behind her.

Elizabeth gently led Mandie over to the cradle where the baby lay, clad only in a diaper and a thin shirt because of the warm weather.

Mandie stood there, silently staring down at him.

Elizabeth looked at her daughter curiously. "Well, aren't you going to say anything?"

Mandie studied the tiny pink wrinkled face and frowned. "He's ugly, Mother," she said without thinking.

"What?" Elizabeth gasped. Then regaining her composure, she spoke gently, choosing her words carefully. "Of course, all newborn babies are wrinkled and may not look very pretty, dear, but I'm sure he's going to grow into a good-looking boy."

"I hope so," Mandie replied.

Elizabeth bent to pick up the baby. "Why don't you hold him, dear?" she said, holding him out to her.

"Oh, no. I don't want to," Mandie protested. Then seeing the hurt look in her mother's eyes, she explained. "I . . . I've never held a tiny baby before. I . . . I just wouldn't know how to hold him. He's too little."

Suddenly the baby burst into tears and screamed at the top of his lungs. Elizabeth cuddled him close and sat down in the rocking chair.

"And now he's crying again," Mandie hollered above the noise.

Mandie watched as her mother cooed to the baby and began rocking him.

"You'll get used to him, dear," Elizabeth told her.

Mandie felt as if she had to get away. "I'll see you after a while." She headed for the door.

"All right, dear. Maybe he'll hush soon," Elizabeth said, still rocking the baby.

Mandie hurried out of the room and raced to her bedroom. The door was open, and she found her bed made and Snowball curled up in the middle of it.

She pounced on the bed and shook up Snowball. "Wake up, you lazy cat," Mandie said. "I need someone to talk to." Playfully, she ruffled his fur, and Snowball immediately started washing his fur back the way it belonged.

Mandie ruffled his coat again, and Snowball looked up at her, confused. He meowed in a sad tone.

Quickly smoothing his fur back into place, she picked him up and hugged him close. "I'm sorry, Snowball," she soothed. "I guess I'm mad at the world and taking it out on you. I'm sorry. I just wish you could talk and tell me what to do." She sighed. "You hear that screaming? That's the new baby trying to burst his lungs, and I can't stand it. Let's go outside."

Jumping up, she quickly left the room with Snowball, hurried downstairs, and ran out into the yard. Since no one was around, she walked out to the summerhouse and sat down.

Deep in thought, she jumped when she heard a voice behind her.

"I heard you got home yesterday."

Mandie turned to see her next-door neighbor Polly Cornwallis stepping into the summerhouse. Polly was the same age as Mandie, and she had also been away at a boarding school—but not the Misses Heathwood's School for Girls in Asheville, North Carolina, which Mandie attended.

"Hello, Polly," Mandie said as her neighbor sat down on the bench opposite her. "You got home the day before I did, didn't you?" Mandie let Snowball down, and he promptly ran away across the lawn.

Polly nodded. "How do you like the new baby?"

"How would *you* like a new baby, Polly, especially one that hollers all the time?" Mandie complained.

"That is a problem," Polly agreed, her black eyes searching Mandie's face. "Is that why you're out here?"

"Of course," Mandie replied. "It's impossible to even think in that house anymore. I couldn't sleep last night."

"Is he sick or something?" Polly asked.

"Or something is right," Mandie said with disgust. "My mother has spoiled him rotten. She holds him and rocks him all the time."

"I do believe I see a spark of jealousy," Polly teased.

Mandie made a face at her friend. "I'm not jealous of him," she insisted. "He's so little and ugly. How could I be?"

"Well, now you're not your mother's only child anymore," Polly reminded her.

Mandie sat up straight. "I am not my mother's *child*," she protested. "I am almost thirteen years old, and that's not a child anymore."

Polly shrugged. "I still consider myself my mother's

child, and I'll soon be thirteen, too," she argued. "Even when I get grown, I'll still be my mother's child."

"Well, go ahead," Mandie said, a little irritated. "Just don't include me in that child business."

Polly tossed her long dark hair as she leaned forward. "I suppose you have a boyfriend back at school, then, if you're so grown up."

"A boyfriend? You know we're too young to even talk about such things," Mandie said.

"I don't think I'm too young. After all, some girls get married at sixteen," Polly reminded her. "When is Joe coming to see you?"

Suddenly Mandie understood what Polly was getting at. Polly was always trying to get Joe to pay attention to her when he came to visit Mandie.

"Whenever he gets ready!" Mandie snapped.

"You know he's going to be fifteen this year on November first," Polly reminded her.

Mandie stood up to shake the wrinkles out of her long skirt. "And what do you mean by that?" she asked, leaning on the rail at the steps.

Polly joined her. "I mean ... that he is definitely old enough to be interested in girls," she replied.

"What does that have to do with the baby?" Mandie asked crossly. "I believe we were discussing the baby, not boyfriends."

"I believe we were discussing both," Polly answered. "But if you'd rather talk about the baby, what are you going to do about him?"

"What do you mean by that?" Mandie asked.

Polly shrugged. "You said you couldn't even think or

sleep or anything because of him, so what's going to happen?" she asked.

"Sooner or later he is going to hush . . ." Mandie said hopefully, "and grow up and quit being a screaming little baby!"

"Don't forget," Polly said, "you'll be long gone from home before he gets grown. You're twelve years older than he is."

Mandie sighed and looked at her neighbor with disgust. "Can't we talk about something besides that baby?"

Polly didn't say anything for a minute. Then finally she said, "I hear you're going to Europe with your grandmother next month."

"That's right." Mandie brightened. "And we're going to be gone a whole month."

"I sure wish I could go," Polly murmured, staring out into space. "Mother says I won't be going for another year or two. She wants me to be old enough to attend some of the social functions over there."

"My friend Celia Hamilton from school is going with us, too," Mandie told her. "You know Celia, don't you? She came here for part of the Christmas holidays, remember?"

"Lucky, lucky, lucky," Polly sighed. "I wonder if my mother will let me take a friend with me when we finally get around to making the trip. Maybe I could even take you."

"I'd like to, but I don't imagine my mother would let me make another trip like that so soon," Mandie replied.

Polly walked down a step. "I've got to go now. My mother is taking me to visit some friends this afternoon, and I have to get ready."

"But it's not even noon yet," Mandie reminded her.

"Oh, but these friends have a good-looking son two years older than I am, and I have to decide what to wear," Polly replied. She started down the pathway, then turned back. "I'll see you tomorrow."

Mandie said goodbye and started back to the house. She had just realized that she couldn't hear the baby hollering. But halfway down the walkway, the screams started up again. Mandie stomped her foot, then turned back to the summerhouse and plopped down on a bench.

"I can't stand it anymore," she said out loud, covering her ears with her hands. "I can't stand all that noise." But where could she go to get away from it?

Suddenly a plan began to form in her head. *I'll just go live with my father's people,* she thought. Her father's mother had been full-blooded Cherokee, and Mandie had lots of Cherokee kinspeople back at Bird-town and Deep Creek. She was sure they would let her stay with them.

Her mother could just keep that howling baby. She didn't want anything to do with him. All she wanted was peace and quiet. She was used to everything being quiet and orderly at school. She just couldn't stand all this racket.

Besides, her mother wouldn't even miss her. Elizabeth was so wrapped up with that baby that she didn't have any time to spend with Mandie anyway. It would be easy to slip out of the house tonight after everyone was in bed.

Mandie bit her lip, remembering her promise to Uncle Ned. Big tears rolled down her cheeks. She just couldn't keep her promise. She had tried, but it was impossible to be happy with that screaming baby. She decided not to even let Uncle Ned know where she was going until she got to her great-uncle's house in Bird-town. Uncle Ned lived at Deep Creek, not far from Bird-town.

When she had first come to her Uncle John's house after her father died, Uncle Ned, Morning Star, and several Indian braves escorted her on the long journey through the mountains and woods by foot.

That was a year ago, she thought. *But I'm sure I could find the way back to Uncle Wirt's house.* It wasn't far from the house where she had lived at Charley Gap with her father and stepmother. After all, Mandie herself was one-fourth Cherokee and she had inherited some of the Indians' skill with direction.

At noon Mandie was still sitting in the summerhouse, thinking and making plans when Liza came to find her. "What you be doin' out heah all by yo'self, Missy?" Liza asked, stepping inside.

"You know why I'm out here," Mandie replied. "Sit down."

Liza shook her head. "Cain't. I come to git you fo' dinnuh," Liza told her. "Yeh, I knows why you be heah instead of in de house. But dat racket gwine stop fo' dinnuh 'cause Miz 'Lizbeth want me to watch dat baby whilst she eats huh dinnuh. I knows how to git dat baby to hush," she said proudly. "All's I has to do is sing real sweet to him and rock him, and he shets up right now."

"Well, thank goodness somebody knows how to hush him." Mandie got up and followed Liza across the lawn to the house. "But, Liza, doesn't that just spoil him that much more?"

"Who care, long as he stop dat howlin' for a little while?" Liza said as she danced on down the lane to the house.

"I wish Mother would let you take care of him all the time then," Mandie suggested.

Liza stopped and turned to face her friend. "Lawsy mercy, Missy. I don't be awantin' to put up wid dat baby all de time. Not me. I likes my job de way it be."

"And I like my house the way it was before that baby came," Mandie said, walking on.

Liza caught Mandie's hand, stopping her in the middle of the path. "But dat baby be yo' bruthuh, and you has to put up wid it."

Mandie looked up at the taller girl and shook her head. "No, I don't have to put up with it," she said. "And I'm not going to."

Liza looked puzzled. "And how're you gwine git out of it?"

Mandie smiled. "I think I've worked out a solution," she said.

Liza eyed her suspiciously. "Like whut? I s'pose you's gwine move up to de third floor o' dis big ol' house."

"I don't think that'd do any good," Mandie argued. "I'd still probably be able to hear him hollering."

Liza shook her head. "I don't think so, Missy. But den all dem spooks live up in de attic, and since you'd have a room all by yo'self, dey'd prob'ly come down and git you."

"Liza!" Mandie scolded. "You know there's no such thing as spooks."

"Jes' you waits till you sees one, den you knows dey's

sech a thing as spooks. Jes' you waits." Liza walked on toward the house.

Mandie followed. "Well, I'm not moving to the third floor anyway," she said.

Liza whirled around. "Missy, whut you be plannin'? You sho' bettuh not be plannin' trouble. Yo' ma ain't in no mood fo' dat."

"I'm not planning trouble, Liza. It's a secret. I can't tell you right now."

Liza put her hands on her hips. "Why cain't you tell me right now?" she demanded. "Heah I always looks aftuh you, and now you gits a secret and won't tell me."

"Maybe later, Liza," Mandie said. "I don't have it all worked out yet."

"Later, humph!" Liza grumbled, continuing on to the house with Mandie following.

After the meal, Elizabeth said she was going to the sun-room to write a few letters as long as the baby was still quiet. Mandie was so tired from her lack of sleep the night before that she decided to go to her room for a nap.

As Mandie approached the sitting room adjoining her mother's bedroom, she walked on tiptoe so she wouldn't wake the baby, unleashing those unbearable screams again. Peeking into the room, she didn't see anyone, so she quietly stepped inside and just stared at the cradle by the window. *Why did this have to happen to me?* she thought. *Everything was just fine until he came along.*

Something drew her toward the cradle, and she walked ever so quietly, hoping not to step on any squeaky floor boards. Soon Mandie towered over the cradle, glaring down at the baby. Her heart beat faster. She clenched

her fists. *Why did he have to ruin everything?* she wondered. Then her thoughts became whispered threats.
"You stupid, stupid baby! I wish you'd never been born!"

"Amanda!" came a hoarse whisper from the doorway.
"What are you saying?"

Chapter 4 / Runaway!

Mandie whirled to see her mother marching toward her. Anger reddened Elizabeth's face as she grabbed Mandie's arm and silently led her out into the hall.

Mandie trembled. She had never seen her mother really angry before. What was Elizabeth going to do?

Her mother closed the door, and the click of the latch woke the baby, setting off another round of ear-splitting screams. For the moment, Elizabeth ignored the baby's cries and concentrated on her daughter.

"Amanda Elizabeth Shaw, what on earth has gotten into you?" she demanded, raising her voice to be heard over the baby's hollering.

Without waiting for an answer Elizabeth raged on. "What a hateful thing to say! I thought we had this jealousy problem all straightened out at Christmastime when I told you I was going to have the baby. But this has gotten way out of hand! What's the matter with you? Why can't you accept that baby and love him as your Uncle John and I do?"

Mandie swallowed hard, and her head felt warm. By

now she barely heard anything Elizabeth was saying. All she wanted to do was to get away from her mother. She thought that she couldn't help how she felt about the baby. But if she talked back, things would only get worse. She didn't know what to do.

"Amanda, I'm speaking to you," her mother persisted.

As the baby continued screaming, Liza raced up the stairs, shot a knowing glance at Mandie, and slipped into the sitting room.

Finally Mandie spoke, fighting back tears. "I'm sorry, Mother, but I can't stand that crying anymore. . . . That baby cries all day, and he screams all night. Nobody can get any sleep. I'm so tired I can hardly keep my head up."

As Mandie talked, behind the sitting room door the baby quieted. Soon Mandie could hear Liza singing softly while the cradle squeaked back and forth.

"I know it's not easy, Amanda. It's not easy on any of us. But you'll get used to it," Elizabeth said, her tone softening.

Mandie shook her head. "I'm not so sure, Mother," she protested. "Why can't you get some help? You and Uncle John have lots of money. Why don't you hire somebody to come and stay here and look after the baby so you can get some rest? Then we could have some time together. And if the baby would stop all that crying, he could rest, too."

"But don't you understand?" Elizabeth sighed. "I want to take care of him myself. I was never able to hold you and rock you and love you when you were born. So I want to enjoy every minute of having him."

Mandie's anger surged through her again. No, her mother had never cared for her when she was a baby.

She never even tried to find out for sure if Mandie had died at birth.

Drawing a deep breath, Mandie attempted to keep her voice steady. "I ... just ... thought ... that would be a good solution to the problem," she said weakly.

"I wish you wouldn't refer to the baby as a *problem*," her mother reprimanded. "He's no problem. He's a joy to have. He'll get over these crying spells soon. And then you and I will have a lot of time together."

Mandie looked down. "It'll never be the same," she mumbled.

"Amanda, that's enough now," Elizabeth scolded. "Why can't you accept that this new baby is a part of our family just as much as you are, and we will all love him?"

Tears filled Mandie's eyes. "I can't!" she cried. "I just can't!" She ran off down the hall to her room, closed the door and locked it, leaning against it from the inside.

As her mother's footsteps approached, big teardrops rolled off Mandie's cheeks onto her dress.

"Open your door, Amanda," her mother said.

Mandie just stood there crying. Again her mother asked her to open the door, but the girl couldn't move.

"Very well, then, you might as well stay in your room for the rest of the day," her mother said firmly. "And I'll tell you something else. Unless your behavior improves, you are *not* going to Europe with your grandmother!"

Mandie threw herself on her bed and sobbed for what seemed like hours. *Mother really doesn't care about me,* she thought. *All she cares about is that screaming baby.*

Now Mandie knew she had to go to Bird-town. And it had to be tonight!

She decided she would wait until midnight to leave. That way all the servants would be asleep. And if her mother was still awake, she would be busy with the baby.

Besides, the full moon would have risen high over the trees by then, and it would be easier to find her way through the dense forests she had to travel through.

Her stomach quivered at the thought of the long, dark paths on the way to Uncle Wirt's house at Bird-town. But then it would be worth the lonely journey to get away from her angry mother and the crying baby. Elizabeth probably wouldn't even miss her.

Mandie walked over and looked out the open window. Snowball, who had been sleeping by the hearth, jumped up and perched on the windowsill beside her.

Mandie reached out and patted his head. "Snowball, you'd better sleep while you can because we have a long walk tonight," she said.

Snowball answered with a meow.

Mandie made a mental list of what she would need to take with her, then flopped down on her bed again for a nap of her own.

When the little ceramic clock on the mantelpiece chimed nine o'clock, Mandie woke and lay on her bed for a few minutes, thinking through her plan to run away. Snowball, who was asleep at her feet, stretched and washed his paws.

Mandie sat up and rubbed her eyes. "Guess I'd better be getting our things together, Snowball," she said with a yawn.

Rummaging through her dresser drawers, she found the flour sack that she had carried her clothes in when she arrived at Uncle John's house the year before. She shook it out. "Now I hope I can find all my old clothes," she said to herself.

She searched through the wardrobe and then the huge drawer at the bottom of it. There she found what she had been looking for—the old navy blue dress she had worn, her old shoes, the only other dress she had owned, and other odds and ends. Beneath the clothes, she found her old school books from Charley Gap.

Sitting down on the floor, she flipped through her books and memories flooded over her. When her father died, she had to live with the Brysons and look after their baby. That child was older than her little brother and was easy to handle. But the Brysons were mean to her and wouldn't let her go to church or to school.

Mandie had learned that she had an uncle, whom she had never known anything about, and she ran away to find him. That was when she brought her meager belongings in the flour sack to Uncle John's house. Her uncle showered her with beautiful clothes and pretty things. But now she would leave all that here. She was going to live with her Cherokee kinspeople, and they didn't possess such finery.

Mandie's conscience tugged at her as she thought of turning her back on Uncle John when he had been so kind to her. But she brushed the thought away.

She pulled out the navy blue dress and held it up to herself. "I wonder if I can get this on," she said as Snowball watched.

Quickly unbuttoning the dress she was wearing, she slipped it off and tried on the old navy blue dress. It was a tight fit, and it was a little short, but she could still wear it. She remembered that the dress had been a little too big the year before when she came there.

Mandie never did care for fine clothes, expensive possessions, and money, so those things weren't hard to leave. It was just Uncle John and her mother—why couldn't her mother understand?—and Aunt Lou and Liza and the others. . . .

The only piece of jewelry she would take was a gold locket her uncle had given her. And she was only taking that because it had her father's picture in it. Taking the necklace out of her jewelry box, she fastened it around her neck, then dropped it out of sight inside the bodice of her dress.

She sat down on the floor and tried on her old cotton stockings. They were still usable, but her old shoes wouldn't even fit on her feet.

"Guess I'll have to wear the ones I had on," Mandie mumbled to herself. "I have too far to go to try walking barefooted." She examined her sensible but expensive leather shoes and put them back on.

As she stood up again, she felt something heavy in the big pocket of her dress. Sticking her hand inside, she brought out the worn New Testament her father had given her before she was even old enough to read.

She knew what was written inside, but she opened it anyway and traced her father's big, scrawling handwriting with her finger. "For my darling daughter, Amanda Elizabeth Shaw," she read. "With all my love forever, Jim Shaw." Tears rushed into her blue eyes, and she closed the book tight, hugging it to her.

"With all my love, forever," Mandie repeated to herself. "Oh, Daddy, I know you loved me with all your heart. If only Mother did."

Suddenly the screams of the baby filled the air. Evidently her mother had opened the windows again. Mandie dropped everything and ran to close all the windows in her room to cut down on the noise. Snowball followed her around.

As she closed the last window, she noticed the big full moon rising through the trees in the distance. "Snowball, the moon is coming up," she told her kitten.

She stopped to think for a moment and then said aloud, "Guess I'd better leave some kind of note so Mother won't worry." Walking over to the little desk in her room, she picked up her school notebook and pulled out a sheet of paper. After some thinking, she wrote, "Gone to live with my Cherokee kinspeople."

Holding up the note to look at it, she said, "I think that's enough. I don't even need to sign it. Mother will know who wrote it."

She carefully laid the sheet of paper in the middle of her bed on the blue silk bedspread. It would be in plain view when someone opened the door to her room.

Mandie stooped and picked up the flour sack. After stuffing into it the few belongings she was taking, she put the rest of her things away in the drawer. Then she went back to sit by the closed window. As she looked out into the darkness, she noticed that the baby's crying had stopped.

She thought through her plan. Everything was packed. All she had to do was take her flour sack and Snowball and slip out of the house at midnight. Mandie wouldn't let herself think about how her mother would feel when she found her gone. She focused on her Cherokee kinspeople. She was positive they would welcome her.

Maybe someday she would come back to her mother—after that baby had grown up enough to stop all that crying. Then her mother would have time for her again.

As Mandie sat there thinking, her eyes began to moisten. She realized that her running away would mean no trip to Europe. She and her grandmother and Celia had been planning this trip for quite some time. Somehow she hoped they would understand.

I should at least write them a letter, telling them I can't go, she thought. Crossing the room, she picked up her notebook, then stopped, setting it down again. Snowball rubbed around her ankles, looking up at her. Mandie picked him up. "I can't write them any letters," she said aloud. "How would I mail them?"

Sighing heavily, she returned to the window and petted her kitten in her lap. "Mother will tell them, I'm sure," she said sadly. "After all, she said if my behavior didn't improve, I couldn't go to Europe anyway."

As Mandie stared out into the darkness, she began to feel hungry. When her mother had confined her to her room, that meant missing supper as well. Lifting her kitten's head, she looked right into his face. "Snowball," she said, "there is one important thing I forgot all about— food! We've got to have some food. It's a long way to Bird-town, and we'll sure get hungry. What will I do?"

She thought a moment, then said, "I know. When we leave, we'll just go through the kitchen and see what we can find to take with us. That way I won't have to go downstairs twice and run the risk of someone seeing me in this old dress."

As Mandie leaned back and waited, her thoughts

churned with questions. What if someone caught her before she even left? What if something happened to her when she was out in the woods all alone? What if her mother sent word to the Cherokees and made her come back?

Mandie wouldn't let herself think about those things.

When the little clock on the mantelpiece struck the midnight hour, Mandie rose and took one good look around the beautiful room she was leaving behind. Then picking up her flour sack and her kitten, she quietly opened the door to the hallway.

There was no sign of a light in any of the rooms, but the full moon shone through the windows in the hallway and on the landing. There was no one in sight.

Mandie held Snowball up to her face and spoke softly into his ear. "We have to be very quiet, Snowball," she whispered.

Snowball rubbed his ear against her face.

Mandie knew where all the creaks in the staircase were so she slowly, carefully made her way down without a sound. Then she hurried into the kitchen. It was even brighter in there because there were more windows to let in the moonlight.

Setting Snowball down on the floor, she put her flour sack on the table and looked through the pie safe. Aunt Lou always put the leftovers in there.

Carefully opening the door, Mandie examined the contents of its shelves. There was one whole pie, probably apple, but that would be too messy to take with her. She also found a large bowl of biscuits and cornbread left from supper. And there was a lot of cheese. Without taking time to look through the other food, she decided on the cheese and the bread.

"What am I going to put it in?" she whispered to herself as she looked around the room.

She spotted Aunt Lou's big white apron hanging on a hook on the back of the door. Quickly taking it down, she spread it out on the table and stacked the bread and cheese in the middle of it. Then she rolled it up and stuck it into her flour sack with her clothes.

Suddenly, Mandie panicked. She couldn't see her kitten anywhere. "Snowball," she called in a whisper, "where are you? Come here." She stooped to look for him.

Just then the kitten darted across the room from the direction of the big fireplace.

Mandie quickly scooped him up, grabbed her flour sack and hurried to the back door. Never stopping for a moment, Mandie ran for the trees at the far side of the yard. Then she made her way on down to the road, staying in the shadows.

Grasping the flour sack with one hand and Snowball with the other, she hurried through the woods. The kitten clung to her dress in fright.

At the edge of town Mandie had to stop to catch her breath. Even though Uncle John's house had disappeared from view long ago, she looked back in the direction she had come. Standing under a huge tree out of the moonlight, she thought about what might happen when someone found her note.

Liza was the one who usually came to wake her for breakfast. Mandie could imagine her running and screaming to Elizabeth with the news.

On the other hand, maybe her mother would come into Mandie's room first. Elizabeth would probably rush to Mr. Bond and demand that he and Abraham get out and find her at once. Mr. Bond probably wouldn't be shocked because he knew that she had run away before to come to her uncle's house.

And when Aunt Lou heard about it, she would probably fuss and fume and say she wished she could get her hands on "her chile."

Mandie knew these were all probablies. She couldn't know what would happen back at Uncle John's house. But she knew one thing for sure. She was going all the way to Bird-town. She was not going to go back.

Chapter 5 / Scary Night!

Mandie walked for hours before she stopped to rest again. When she came upon a clearing in the middle of the thick woods, she found a big old log that made a comfortable seat in the bright moonlight.

Of course Snowball wanted down the minute Mandie stopped, but she was afraid to release him. He might run away.

"You can't get down, Snowball," Mandie told him.

Still the white kitten squirmed and squirmed, trying to get loose. Figuring he would sit still to eat, she opened her flour sack, unrolled Aunt Lou's apron, and broke off a hunk of cheese. Laying the cheese on the log beside her, she set the kitten next to it. Snowball sniffed the cheese and immediately began eating.

As she started to roll the apron back up, she noticed that it had unusually long apron strings because Aunt Lou was so large. Suddenly she had an idea. "Forgive me, Aunt Lou," she said into the air, quickly ripping the strings from the apron. "I'll get you another one someday, some-how. I promise."

Then knotting the strings together, Mandie fashioned a kind of harness and leash and slipped it around her kitten's neck. Snowball didn't fight it because he was too busy eating.

"Hurry up, Snowball," she urged. "You should have had that little old piece of cheese eaten by now."

As Mandie nibbled on some cheese and bread that she had kept out for herself, she jumped at every little sound in the woods.

"I know what I'm doing is not exactly right," she told Snowball. It was the first time she even admitted it to herself. "But what *is* the right thing to do in a situation like this? My mother is so wrapped up in that baby she doesn't have time for me anymore. After she gets over the shock of finding me gone, I'm sure she won't mind too much."

She ran her hand over Snowball's back. "Besides," she continued, "I just can't stand that screaming day and night. There must be something wrong with that baby to make him yell like that. I don't know how my mother stands it."

Suddenly a slight sound caught Mandie's ear. She thought she heard a twig snap and some leaves rustle. She quickly glanced around the clearing. Grabbing her kitten and her flour sack, she held her breath and waited for another noise, hoping it wouldn't come.

So softly that no one could have heard her, Mandie tried to comfort herself with her favorite Bible verse. "What time I am afraid I will put my trust in thee," she whispered. Then she drew a deep breath.

Somehow Snowball managed to pull free from her hand and jump down. Immediately he started wriggling to get free from the harness. Mandie held tight to the other end of the leash.

She reached down and picked up her white kitten. "Come on, Snowball. We've got to get a move on," she whispered.

As soon as the kitten finished eating, Mandie untied the harness and stuck it in her pocket. "We need to be a long, long way from home by sunup. Hold on to my shoulder and we'll get going."

Looking around, Mandie decided they were far enough away now to leave the woods and follow the banks of the Little Tennessee River. This would take her directly through Charley Gap, where she had lived with her father. Besides, she would feel safer out of the woods, so she could see any possible danger.

Tired, and still hungry, Mandie traipsed along the river for miles and miles. Then, although the log cabin her father had built was not exactly on her route to Bird-town, Mandie veered away from the river and headed toward the farm.

Determinedly, she forced her weary feet to carry her on. Once in a while she put the harness back on Snowball to let him walk, but each time, he wiggled and thrashed around so badly that she gave up trying to keep him on a leash.

At daybreak, she stood on top of a mountain and stopped to watch the sun come up far, far away. This was her favorite time of day, the time when everything was rested—except her now—and a whole new day lay before her.

In the yellow-orange colors of the dawn, Mandie thrilled at the beauty of nature. The birds chattered to each other, and in the distance Mandie could hear a cow mooing. The dew covered the leaves and the underbrush, and her dress became damp as she pushed her way through the thickets.

As she trudged on, the sun rose high in the sky and the air became warmer. Finally, as she reached the top of a familiar mountain, she peered down to see the small log cabin that was her former home.

Mandie's heart beat faster. She started down the mountain, cuddling her kitten close. "Now you be quiet, Snowball," she cautioned softly. "We don't want anyone to see us. We're only going to walk by and look."

Snowball meowed in response.

As Mandie crept nearer the log cabin, floods of memories blurred her eyes with tears. She wiped them away quickly and looked around. A flock of chickens chased around the yard, and cows mooed in the pasture, but there was no one in sight.

Stopping behind the huge chestnut tree that stood at the edge of the yard, Mandie whispered to Snowball. "This used to be our home," she said. "You probably can't remember it because you were just a tiny kitten when we left."

Her voice broke and she looked toward the sky. *Oh, dear God,* she cried in her heart, *if only we could live here again! If only I could see my daddy again and talk to him one more time!*

She wiped her eyes with the back of her hand. "I thank you for all the fine clothes, the beautiful home back in Franklin, and all that good food. But I would trade it all for this one simple log cabin, dear Lord, if I could just be with my daddy again."

A noise nearby interrupted Mandie's prayer. Quickly regaining her composure, she slipped back among the trees. *It might just be an animal,* she thought, but she couldn't take any chances. She waited silently for a few minutes but didn't hear anything else.

Stepping out of a clump of bushes for one last look at the log cabin, she took a deep breath. Then she turned toward the mountain to go to the cemetery where her father was buried.

As the path grew steep, Mandie stopped for a moment. Setting down the flour sack and her kitten, she tucked the hem of her long skirt into the waistband to get it out of her way. Climbing over the rough rocks and boulders ahead of her would be hard enough without tripping on her skirt.

Nearing the summit of the mountain, she found clusters of bright Indian Paintbrush blooming along the way. Halting once more, she gathered a handful of the blooms, tucked them in the fold of her upturned skirt, and went on.

At the top, she was completely exhausted. It took every ounce of her strength to stumble over to her father's grave. Fresh flowers in a jar full of water stood by the head marker.

Mandie looked around her. There were no weeds over the grave, and the grass had been trimmed. She smiled through the tears that started to come. "Joe *has* kept his promise to look after it for me," she said, adding the Indian Paintbrush to the jar of fresh flowers.

As memories of her father filled her mind, Mandie fell to the ground weeping, heedless of the kitten who had finally won his freedom. "Oh, Daddy, I loved you so

66

much!" she cried, burying her face in her arms. "So much!" She sobbed uncontrollably as Snowball rubbed against her shoulder.

Totally exhausted from the long night's journey and overcome with grief, Mandie lay there on the grass and cried herself to sleep.

The next thing Mandie knew, Snowball was pushing against her arm. She woke with a start and rolled over, shading her eyes from the glare of the sun. "Oh, Snowball." She grabbed for her kitten and propped herself up on one elbow. "How long have I been asleep?"

Snowball stretched and meowed.

Mandie glanced up. Judging from the sun's position in the sky, she guessed it had not been long. Jumping to her feet, she untucked the hem of her skirt and shook it out. "Snowball, we need to get going. Come here."

The kitten led her in a chase around the cemetery, then stopped next to the flour sack just long enough for his mistress to grab him. "Snowball!" Mandie scolded. "We don't have time to play around. We've still got a long journey ahead of us. Now you behave."

Snowball meowed in reply and clung to the shoulder of Mandie's dress as she snatched up the flour sack and hurried down the mountain. The path that would take them back to the river and on to Bird-town led through the woods. Before they had gone very far, Mandie's stomach growled loudly. She suddenly realized that she hadn't eaten anything since that bite of cheese and bread during the night.

Finding a place where the bushes and underbrush weren't quite so thick, she sat down on the ground and took out their food. As soon as Snowball smelled it, he began meowing and rubbing against her hands.

"Wait, Snowball," she scolded. "I know you're hungry. I'm hurrying, but I can't get you anything to eat if you keep getting in my way." Breaking off a small hunk of cheese she set it on the ground for him. "Now behave yourself and don't run off while I eat," she said.

Snowball looked up at his mistress and meowed, then began eating his food.

Keeping an eye out for danger, Mandie ate quickly. As she finished her food, she looked over at her kitten, who was licking his paws. "Let's go, Snowball," she said. "We have to find some water." Picking up her flour sack, she reached for him, but he darted off and disappeared into the woods.

"Snowball, come back here!" Mandie yelled, racing after him. "Here, kitty, kitty. Snowball, where are you?" she called as she searched the bushes. There was not a sound in reply.

Once again tears filled her blue eyes. "Snowball, where are you? Please don't be lost!" she cried.

Suddenly, she heard Snowball's angry growl close by. Mandie crept forward, trying to locate him without being seen. She didn't want him running off again.

Then she heard another growl, louder this time. She looked off to the right and saw Snowball with his fur standing up, his back arched.

Mandie eased forward, then froze. Directly in front of Snowball a huge snake stood coiled, ready to strike. Mandie recognized the brown and gold markings of a deadly timber rattler. Her heart pounded. What should she do? The snake could strike at any minute.

If she yelled at Snowball to run, the startled snake

would surely strike. Mandie was afraid to move an inch. Feeling drained of all her strength, she could hardly breathe.

Snowball growled again and swiped his paw in the air. The snake hissed and moved its head.

Mandie had to do something. That snake was going to kill her kitten. Racing forward, she snatched up Snowball by the scruff of his neck and flew down the path as fast as her feet could carry her.

She heard the snake moving behind her but didn't dare look back. "Please help us, dear God," she prayed. Out of breath, she could say no more, but she kept running for a long time.

Finally, as they came to the river, she got a catch in her side and stumbled to a halt. She fell to the ground just inches from the water. Snowball meowed and reached over and brushed his head against his mistress's face.

Unable to say anything, Mandie just smiled. She was sure that her kitten was thanking her for saving him from the deadly snake. After washing her face in the shallow water of the riverbank, Mandie let Snowball drink. Then she picked up her flour sack, and they continued on their way.

"Thank you, dear God. Thank you," she murmured as she followed the riverbank.

Before long she came to more woods that grew thick right down to the river's edge. There was no way to avoid them and not much of a path going through. Mandie struggled to push heavy limbs out of her way, and briars kept snagging her long, full skirt.

"There must have been a better way to go, but I just

don't know where," Mandie said. Clutching Snowball, she hurried on. "I sure hope there's not much more of this." It was hard to believe it could be so dark in the woods when the sun shone so brightly overhead.

Snowball didn't try to get down, but he meowed every time they ran into a limb. There were so many branches running every which way, it was impossible to dodge them all. Mandie tried to shield her face, but she kept getting scratched.

All at once her head snapped back. She was stuck! Glancing back over her shoulder, she saw that her long blond braid had gotten tangled in a prickly branch. Afraid to let Snowball down, she dropped her flour sack and tried to free herself with one hand.

Suddenly, she noticed small animals scattering and birds taking flight as if startled. Then she had the strange feeling she was being watched. Turning her head in the other direction, she gasped.

Two young Indian men stood, partially hidden in the brush, watching her.

Mandie's heart skipped a beat, and she clutched Snowball tightly. "Are y'all Cherokees?" she asked hopefully.

The two Indians looked at each other and mumbled something that didn't sound like the Cherokee language. Then they started toward her, their faces serious.

Mandie bit her lip and frantically tried to free herself from the prickly branch.

The Indians tramped through the brush and stood in front of her, their dark eyes boring into hers.

Mandie's heart thumped loudly. *What do they want?* she wondered.

The Indians looked at each other and mumbled something again. Then the shorter of the two grabbed Mandie's flour sack and rummaged through it. Turning to the other man, he shrugged.

Mandie trembled in suspense. These Indians obviously weren't Cherokees. But were they friendly or hostile? If only they spoke English . . . So far they hadn't tried to harm her, but could they be trusted?

Snowball dug his claws into the shoulder of Mandie's dress.

Mandie struggled again, trying to free her long blond braid from the branch.

Suddenly the two Indians started toward her. Mandie froze. The taller Indian extended both hands, pointing to Mandie's neck. Her heart beat wildly. She cringed.

Then the Indian reached behind her and began to loosen her blond braid from the prickly branch that held her in its grasp. With the Indian's face only inches from her own, she hardly dared to breathe. But in seconds he had freed her, and she collapsed on the ground with relief.

The Indians helped her up, their eyes filled with concern.

Somehow Mandie managed a weak smile. "Th-thank you," she stammered. "Thank you very much." She still felt faint.

The Indians patted her gently on the back and mumbled something in their language.

"Snowball, I think we'd better get going again," Mandie said, grabbing her flour sack.

Grateful, but still not sure of the Indians, she waved to them as she headed off. "Goodbye," she called over her shoulder.

She didn't want to look back, but she could feel their eyes on her, watching until she came to a curve in the path. When she was sure she was out of their sight, she finally started to relax. "Whew!" She let out her breath noisily. "That was a close call," she said to her pet. "You didn't like them, either, did you, Snowball?"

The white kitten looked up at her and meowed.

Chapter 6 / Dangers!

Mandie trudged on, and some time later her weary, blistered feet brought her to the Tomahawk Trail where it crossed the Little Tennessee River. Following that trail, she came to the Tuckasegee River.

Mandie surveyed the shallow part of the river where she would cross on a foot bridge. "Snowball, let's get into the water and cool off," she suggested.

As Mandie hurried down the bank, Snowball jumped out of her arms and ran ahead of her. Sitting down on the bank, Mandie took off her shoes and watched Snowball dip his paw in the flowing water as he drank. Then he shook his head to get the water off his whiskers.

Mandie tucked up her long skirt and waded out into the cool river. "Oh, Snowball, this feels so good," she called back to him at the edge. "Come on, get in the water."

As she waded back toward the bank, she reached out for him. Snowball tried to escape her grasp, but the pebbles he was sitting on scattered under his weight, and he tumbled into the water.

Tired and full of tension, Mandie started to giggle, then burst into gales of silly laughter as she watched. She knew he could swim, so she wasn't worried about that. The kitten managed to right himself in the water and tried paddling back toward the riverbank. But the current was too strong for him.

When Mandie finally reached him, she patted his wet head. "Come on, Snowball. Let's have some fun." She tried to coax him to follow her, but he kept treading water and violently shaking his head to clear his ears.

He looked up at his mistress with sad eyes. "Meow!" he whimpered.

"All right, you silly kitten," Mandie finally gave in. "Come here. I'll hold you."

As though he could understand what she was saying, Snowball immediately paddled his way toward his mistress. Mandie snatched him up and shook him gently to get rid of some of the water. His fur stuck to him, and he wiggled his ears, trying to get the water out of them.

"Oh, Snowball, you look pitiful," Mandie said. Holding his drenched little body close, she rubbed her face against the wet fur. "I'm sorry you fell in, Snowball," she told him. "I'll get you dried off."

Stepping out onto the sand of the riverbank, she hurried to get Aunt Lou's apron out of her flour sack. After putting the remaining food back in the sack, she sat down in the dirt and used the apron as a towel to dry her kitten. Snowball didn't protest.

"All right, that's the best I can do," she said after a few minutes. "You finish." She released the kitten, saying, "Now I have to dry my feet."

While Snowball licked his paws, Mandie rubbed her

own feet with the wet apron and tugged her stockings and shoes back on.

Suddenly Mandie heard the sound of horses and a wagon in the distance. She looked up. Downriver, she saw a rig crossing the bridge. It was headed in the direction of Bird-town. Mandie jumped up. Sure that it was a Cherokee wagon, she started waving Aunt Lou's white apron and yelling.

She squinted and shaded her eyes from the sun. She couldn't tell who was driving. The wagon was too far away. But to her surprise, after it reached the other side of the river, it turned and came toward her.

Snatching up Snowball and the flour sack, Mandie raced across the foot bridge toward the wagon. She reached the other side just in time to see who was driving.

"Tsa'ni!" she cried, recognizing her troublesome cousin.

The Indian boy was Uncle Wirt Pindar's grandson. He lived in Deep Creek, near Uncle Ned.

Tsa'ni hated white people and had a way of making life miserable for Mandie. But she was desperate for a ride. Tired and hungry, she didn't know how she would ever make it the rest of the way before dark.

Her Cherokee cousin stopped the wagon beside her. Eyeing her curiously, he smirked. "What are you doing out here all alone?" he asked. "You and that white cat?"

He scowled at her tucked-up skirt.

Embarrassed that her legs were showing, Mandie dropped the hem of her skirt and straightened the folds. "Tsa'ni, I am on the way to Uncle Wirt's house," she explained. "Would you please give me a ride the rest of the way?"

"I am not going to Bird-town," Tsa'ni said curtly. "I am going home to Deep Creek. Why do you want to see my grandfather? Why do you not stay at home with that white woman who is your mother?"

Mandie didn't want to start an argument. "I just want to visit your grandfather for awhile," she said. "School is out for the summer, and my mother is home with her new baby. Please, Tsa'ni, couldn't you go around by Uncle Wirt's and drop me off there?"

"How did you get this far?" Tsa'ni sneered. "By yourself?"

"Well, yes. I'm alone," she admitted reluctantly, knowing her cousin would be suspicious of that.

"Oh, so your mother does not know you are here," he said. "Go back to your white people. That is where you belong." Whipping the horses, he sped off down the road.

As Mandie stared after him, her eyes filled with tears. Why was Tsa'ni always so mean to her? After all, he was blood kin—actually her second cousin.

Mandie hugged Snowball and flopped down on the sand. She sighed deeply. "Well, Snowball, we can't afford to waste time just sitting here," she said. "Let's eat a bite while we're stopped. Then we've got to keep going."

Snowball washed himself while Mandie opened the flour sack and took out the remaining bread and cheese. Saving a little bit for later and sharing some with Snowball, she ate hurriedly, then walked on again. They still had a long way to go before they reached Uncle Wirt's house.

Refreshed from wading in the river, Mandie started out quickly, but soon weariness set in again. As the day wore on, her weary steps grew slower and slower. She had to stop and rest more often.

In open areas, the sun was scorching hot. Mandie found herself hurrying through the clearings and taking her time through the cool, dark woods.

Then as she came over the crest of a steep, wooded mountain, she stopped, paralyzed with fear. There, right in front of her, stood a huge bear.

"Oh, no!" Mandie gasped. Her heart beat wildly.

Snowball dug his claws into her shoulder.

Startled, the bear reared and stood on his hind feet. Mandie held her breath. Those beady little eyes threatened.

Hardly able to form the words, Mandie once again repeated her silent prayer, "What time I am afraid I will put my trust in thee."

Snowball arched his back and hissed.

The huge bear growled and started toward them.

He's about to attack! Mandie panicked. *I've got to distract him somehow!* she thought. Then she remembered the bread and cheese. Fumbling desperately with the flour sack, she found the remaining food and tossed it as hard as she could, just off the path by the bear.

Watching it land, the huge animal ambled over to investigate.

Mandie raced past him, clutching Snowball tightly as she hurried down the mountainside. In fear and exhaustion, she stumbled along. Her feet slid on rocks, her hair caught in branches and limbs, and briars snagged her clothes. But she couldn't stop. She had to get as far away from that bear as possible.

Snowball protested loudly at the jarring ride and dug his claws into her again.

As Mandie neared the bottom of the mountain, her feet slipped on a moss-covered rock, and she slid the rest of the way, scraping her legs and elbows. Snowball jumped free. And Mandie, skidding and tumbling the last few feet, tried to brace herself, but she landed squarely in front of a wagon traveling on the road below.

"Whoa!" the driver shouted.

The two horses reared up as the driver brought the wagon to a sudden stop a few inches from where Mandie lay.

Mandie couldn't move. The driver jumped down from the wagon and ran to her side. She couldn't say anything.

The man bent over her with concern. "Are you all right, young lady?" he asked, breathing hard. "Are you hurt badly?"

Mandie detected a strange accent. She tried to smile as the man offered to help her up. Still clutching her flour sack, she got weakly to her feet.

"I . . . I'm all right," she finally managed to say, breathing a silent word of thanks to God. Mandie studied the man curiously. He looked young but was dressed in a well-worn black suit and hat. Out here in the country, not many men wore suits except to church, and this wasn't Sunday.

The man brushed some leaves and grass from Mandie's back as Snowball rubbed around her ankles. "Do you live around here? Could I give you a ride home, perhaps?" he offered.

"No," Mandie answered hesitantly. "You see I'm on my way to my great-uncle's house at Bird-town."

The stranger's bright blue eyes stared at her. He seemed to be trying to figure out what was going on.

Curly red hair showed beneath his black hat. "That is quite a ways from here," he said. "However, I'm going in that direction. Could I give you a ride?"

"But I don't know you," Mandie said slowly. She stared at the man, whose blue eyes and red hair reminded her of her beloved father.

"Oh, I'm sorry, young lady," the man apologized. "I should introduce myself. I'm Riley O'Neal from Boston, and I have come south to minister to the heathen Indians, and—"

Mandie put her hands on her hips. "The Indians are not heathens," she protested. "I happen to be one-fourth Cherokee myself." She drew herself up tall.

"Oh, dear. I didn't mean to offend you," Riley O'Neal replied. "I have never been south before, but our church in Boston is under the impression that there are quite a few Indians here who know nothing about Christianity. I have been sent as a missionary to set up a school for them."

Mandie looked at him suspiciously. "I don't think they need your school," she said. "They already have their own churches and Sunday schools."

"But we are planning to set up what you might call a 'reading, writing, and arithmetic school,'" he explained. "And we can teach them about God at the same time."

"The ones who want to can go to the white schools," Mandie argued. "Most of them aren't interested in that kind of education. They have their own language and customs."

"But as I understand it, they have to travel quite a distance to the 'white schools,' as you call them. We would like to build a school right in the Cherokee village."

Mandie wasn't sure what to say about that.

The man went on. "It's getting late," he said. "Why don't you get in the wagon, and I'll take you to your uncle's house. Then I can tell you all about our schools on the way."

Mandie hesitated. How could she be sure this man really was a missionary? She had always been taught that it could be dangerous to go off with strangers. Silently she asked God to make the decision for her. Should she trudge on by foot or should she accept the ride? She was terribly worn out and she ached from her fall.

The man saw her hesitation. "Just a minute," he said. Hurrying back to the wagon, he reached inside a valise and pulled out a sheaf of papers to show her.

"This is my identification," he said, showing her several certificates and official-looking documents with his name on them. "I'm glad to see that you have good sense about becoming involved with strangers."

As he unfolded one large paper and held it out, he said, "This is my commission from my church to start the school. Here are my name and address." Mandie noticed the paper read *Reverend* Riley O'Neal. He looked young to be a preacher. Then rummaging through the untidy stack of papers, he produced a picture. "And see? This is a tintype of myself and the members of my church back in Boston."

Mandie nodded. "Thank you," she said. "I believe you are who you say you are." Then with a little laugh, she added, "In fact, you'd better be because all the Cherokees in these mountains would come to my rescue if anything happened to me."

The missionary folded the papers. "Yes, they are your

relatives, aren't they?" he replied with a smile.

"I'm sorry for my harsh words before," Mandie apologized. "Please forgive me. I guess I'm not very grateful for a ride, am I? I'm just awfully tired and hungry. So is Snowball." She picked up her pet and stroked his fur.

The missionary looked down at the white kitten. "Oh, I was so worried about you that I didn't even notice your cat," he said with a little laugh. "Well, let's get the two of you to your uncle's house, then."

Mandie followed the man to the wagon, and he helped her up on the seat.

Jumping up beside her, the missionary returned the papers to the valise and urged the horses on. He glanced at her dirty, torn dress and the tangled blond hair escaping from its long braid. "You must have come a long way then," he said.

"I have," she agreed. But she hoped he wouldn't pursue the matter. He was asking dangerous questions, and she didn't want him to know the truth about her journey.

"Where do you live, Miss . . . ah . . . I don't believe you told me your name," he said with a smile.

"Amanda Shaw," she replied, suddenly wishing she had made up a name. "I'm going to live with my Uncle Wirt."

"Is he Cherokee?" the missionary asked.

"Oh, yes. Uncle Wirt is a full-blooded Cherokee," Mandie answered proudly. "You see, my grandmother was his sister." Mandie tried to change the subject. "Tell me about the school you plan to begin," she said, rubbing Snowball's fur. "Will it be on the Cherokee reservation?"

"That depends on a lot of things," the missionary replied. "I understand there are many Cherokees who don't live on the reservation."

"Yes, lots of them live at Deep Creek. That's where my father's friend, Uncle Ned, lives," Mandie explained.

The wagon suddenly lurched on the rough road. "Does your father live there also?" the man asked.

"My father is . . . is not living anymore," Mandie said, unable to bring herself to say the word *dead*.

"The Lord rest his soul," the missionary said. "I'm sorry. I seem to be saying all the wrong things." After a few moments he continued. "I suppose you know all the Cherokee Indians in these mountains, am I correct?"

"Goodness no!" she exclaimed. "There are hundreds of Cherokees, probably thousands. Besides, I only found out last year that I'm part Cherokee. And my mother sent me off to Asheville to a girls' school right after that, so I haven't had much time to meet all my Indian relatives." Again, she wished she wouldn't talk so much. She was giving away too much personal information.

"So your mother is still living, then, is that right?"

"Well, yes, she's living, but I'm going to live with my great-uncle, at least for the summer." She fidgeted with the flour sack by her side.

Riley O'Neal looked at her again. "Uh-huh," he said.

The way he said it, Mandie was sure he had figured out that she was running away from home. *Oh, so what?* she finally decided. *There's nothing he can do about it.*

The young missionary cleared his throat. "I'm glad you'll be living with the Indians," he told her with a smile. "You seem to be well educated. Perhaps you could help me get the school started."

Mandie frowned. "I don't know about that. I'm already having a hospital built for them—actually there are workmen doing the construction. I'm just furnishing the gold to pay for it."

The man looked at her in disbelief.

"You see, my friends and I found a pile of gold in an old cave a while back," she explained. "And that's the gold that's paying for the hospital."

"You found real gold in a cave?"

Mandie explained how they had discovered the gold and her idea about building a hospital when the Cherokees refused to claim the gold.

"That is a wonderful thing to be doing for the Indians," the missionary said. "The Lord will bless you for that."

As they talked on, Mandie finally caught sight of a cluster of Cherokee log cabins down the road. "Look!" She pointed. "We're not far from Uncle Wirt's house now."

Then all of a sudden she began to worry. How was she going to explain why she was here?

Riley O'Neal looked around at the neat cornfields and the rows of log cabins. "So this is Bird-town," he said, driving slowly on.

"Yes. My Uncle Wirt lives on down a ways," Mandie replied. "I'll show you."

As dusk settled over the little village, the aroma of food cooking filled the air. Mandie's stomach growled, and Snowball sat up in her lap and sniffed. Several Indians were walking around in their yard and along the road. Mandie guessed that they had probably already eaten their evening meal.

"Here." She pointed quickly to the largest house in the center of the community. "Uncle Wirt lives here. He—" She stopped short as she noticed Tsa'ni jump into a wagon by Uncle Wirt's front door. She scowled. How could he have been so mean as to lie about where he was going?

The missionary pulled his wagon into the yard just as Tsa'ni drove by on Mandie's side. Her cousin eyed her companion curiously.

"You told me you weren't coming to Bird-town," Mandie yelled at him.

"I changed my mind," the Indian boy replied. Whipping the horses, he raced off down the road.

"He lied," Mandie mumbled to herself.

The missionary pulled the horses to a stop near the big cabin. "He told a lie? Is that what you said?"

"Yes," Mandie said angrily, preparing to jump down from the wagon. Then she turned around and quickly explained what had happened at the Tuskasegee River.

"Your cousin is one of those people we'd like to help with our ministry," Riley O'Neal replied. He jumped down from the wagon and walked around to help Mandie.

But Mandie was too quick for him. She had already stepped down. No matter how much the Misses Heathwood's School for Girls tried to teach her about being ladylike, she was used to doing things for herself.

"Thank you, Mr. O'Neal, for giving me a ride," she said, smiling up into the missionary's pleasant face. Mandie expected him to get back into the wagon and drive off, but he just stood there. Suddenly she realized that he intended to go in and meet her relatives. She fidgeted with her flour sack nervously.

Mandie knew her Uncle Wirt and his family were members of a Christian church, and she was not sure as to how they might react to this young fellow coming in and trying to start something new. Besides, she didn't really want him around when she told her relatives why she had come. It was going to be hard enough as it was.

Riley O'Neal patiently waited for Mandie to turn toward the house.

"I have to warn you," Mandie began as they started to the door. "I'm not sure what my Cherokee kinspeople will think of you."

The missionary smiled. "We're all children of God, aren't we now?"

Mandie smiled up at him. "Of course we are." Looking ahead, she saw Uncle Wirt and Aunt Saphronia standing in the doorway waiting for them. "Come on. I'll introduce you," she said.

As she neared the doorway, she saw the curious, worried expressions on their faces. *Oh, things are going to be complicated,* she thought.

Chapter 7 / Cherokee Kinspeople

As Mandie and Riley O'Neal approached Uncle Wirt and Aunt Saphronia in the doorway, neither of the old people said a word.They just glanced from Mandie to the missionary and back again.

"Uncle Wirt, Aunt Saphronia, this is Mr. O'Neal," Mandie began. "He gave me a ride to your house."

The missionary extended his hand, but Uncle Wirt did not take it. He just stared at the young man.

"He's a missionary, Mr. Wirt," Mandie explained. "He tells stories from the Big Book like the minister in your church does. Brother O'Neal is one of God's preachers."

Uncle Wirt and Aunt Saphronia exchanged glances, then looked the missionary over.

"Where from?" Uncle Wirt asked.

"Way up north in Boston," Riley O'Neal answered. "A long, long way from here."

"Why you come see Cherokees?" the old Indian asked.

Mandie quickly spoke for the missionary. "He wants to build a school for the Cherokee people, Uncle Wirt," she explained.

"School? Cherokees go to school," Uncle Wirt argued.

"We understand there are a lot of Cherokees who don't attend school because it's too far away," Riley O'Neal said. "We want to help them learn to read and write and do arithmetic—and also learn God's Word."

"Cherokees not have books to read," the old Indian replied. "Not need learn write. No pen. No paper. No money to count."

"But we plan to make things better for your people," the missionary argued. "We will give you books and pens and paper and also Bibles." He smiled broadly. "And with an education and religion the Cherokees will become richer, better people."

Mandie held her breath. Uncle Wirt would take that as an insult. She knew he considered the Cherokees the best people in the world.

Uncle Wirt stood silent for a moment. Then he stepped aside and motioned to the missionary. "Come. My house welcome preacher. We talk."

"Thank you, sir," the missionary replied, as he stepped inside the big log cabin. "I'm honored." He took off his black hat and held it in his hand.

Snowball jumped down, and Mandie turned to embrace her great-aunt, a tiny woman with a million wrinkles. Snowball raced over to the pan of scraps on the hearth that the elderly couple put out for their own cats. The white kitten ate hungrily.

Aunt Saphronia silently smiled at Mandie and took her by the hand to the long table where the two men already sat across from each other. The pleasant aroma from good Cherokee cooking lingered in the air. Mandie and her great-aunt seated themselves at the other end of the table and listened.

"Your school good for all Cherokees?" Uncle Wirt asked.

"I promise you, sir, we will have the best-qualified teachers and the most modern books," he told the Indian proudly, "and we'll prepare the Cherokees to make a better living. They will learn the ways of the white man and find out how to do business with him."

"White man not want to do business with Cherokee," the old Indian protested. "White man not always right."

"You're correct, sir," the missionary continued. "The white man is not always right. For instance, the white man took the Indians' land and moved them out. That was not morally right. That's why the Cherokees must learn the white man's ways, so they can protect themselves against any future happenings like this."

"Cherokees learn too late. Nothing left," Uncle Wirt said sadly. "Nothing left for white man to take."

Riley O'Neal smiled sympathetically. "If the Cherokees learn things the white man knows, then the Cherokees will be able to get work and make money and live better," he said. "And if they learn to read, they can read God's Word for themselves. With the Lord's help anything is possible."

Mandie smiled at the missionary's optimistic spirit.

"Where make school?" Uncle Wirt asked, pushing back his long silver-streaked black hair.

Mandie leaned forward, listening eagerly. She knew a good place.

"Wherever the most convenient place would be for the Cherokees," Riley O'Neal replied. "Since I'm not yet familiar with your area, maybe you could choose the place."

Mandie leaned forward. "What about building it near the hospital, Uncle Wirt?" she asked excitedly. "That area has already been cleared to make a road to it."

"Maybe," Uncle Wirt said thoughtfully. "We have powwow. Cherokee talk. Maybe school. Maybe not school." He rose.

"Thank you, sir," the missionary said, also standing. Once again he extended his hand, and this time Uncle Wirt shook it heartily.

Aunt Saphronia came over to stand beside her husband. "Eat," she offered.

Uncle Wirt turned to the missionary and nodded. "Put horse in barn. Eat," he said. "Come."

"Why, thank you," the missionary replied in surprise.

As the men left the cabin, Mandie followed her great-aunt to the cupboard. The old woman started taking down dishes.

Mandie glanced at the big, covered iron kettles hanging in the fireplace. "Have y'all had your supper, Aunt Saphronia," she asked. "Something sure smells good."

The old woman shook her head. "We eat when you eat."

Mandie smiled, grateful that neither of her relatives had asked her about her unexpected visit. She went back to the bucket of water by the back door and dipped some into a washbin to wash her dirty, scraped-up hands before eating.

There was only friendly conversation during the meal. Uncle Wirt and the missionary did most of the talking. And Mandie was pleased to see the young man trying to learn as much as he could about the Cherokee people and their customs.

Exhausted and starving, Mandie hurriedly ate the tasty stew set before her, then had a second helping. But she was so tired, she couldn't hold her head up.

She looked over at Snowball, asleep on the hearth by the fire. The Cherokees kept fires going in their huge fireplaces all year-round because they cooked their meals in kettles that hung over the flames. Some foods took days to cook over a low fire.

When the meal was over, the missionary stood up and thanked the Indian couple for their hospitality. "The food was delicious," he said sincerely. "But it's getting late, and I must be finding a place to stay."

The others also stood.

Uncle Wirt placed his hand on the missionary's shoulder. "Stay here," he offered. "Bed up ladder." He pointed to a ladder nearby that disappeared into a loft above.

The missionary hesitated. "Only if you allow me to pay you," he said.

Anger clouded Uncle Wirt's old, wrinkled face.

Mandie could see that this was just the first of the clashes between Cherokee ways and white men's ways. She quickly spoke up. "Please understand. My Uncle Wirt is offering you hospitality. Since he has welcomed you to his house, he would be highly insulted if you insisted on paying for it."

Uncle Wirt smiled at Mandie. "Papoose learning ways of our people," he said.

The young man quickly apologized. "I ... I'm ... so sorry," he stammered. "It's just that ... I'm on an allowance from my church, and I ... I thought perhaps ...

perhaps you could use a little extra money."

"Not need money!" Uncle Wirt replied emphatically. "Money not buy food and bed in my house."

"I apologize. Please forgive me," the young missionary said, thrusting his hands deep into his pockets. "I gratefully accept your offer."

Uncle Wirt nodded his approval. "Two rooms up ladder," he told him. "One for you. One for Papoose."

"Thank you, sir," Riley O'Neal said. "Now, would you please excuse me for a little while? I'd like to take a short walk to commune with my Savior."

The old Indian smiled. "Go. I talk to Papoose."

As the missionary went outside, Uncle Wirt turned to Mandie and indicated the cleared-off end of the long table. "Sit," he ordered.

Sensing the sternness in the old man's voice, she quickly obeyed.

Uncle Wirt looked over at Aunt Saphronia, who was scuttling about, trying to clean up the supper dishes. "Come," he called.

The little old woman instantly put down the dishes and hurried to her husband's side. Together they sat down across the table from Mandie.

Mandie knew what that meant. They weren't joining forces with her until they found out exactly what was going on and why she had suddenly shown up at their house. But she was surprised when Uncle Wirt spoke.

"Tsa'ni say he see Papoose near river. No one with her," he began in a firm voice.

"Tsa'ni? I might have known," Mandie groaned. "I tried to get him to give me a ride here to your house, but he said he wasn't coming this way. Then when I got here,

I saw him drive off in a wagon."

Aunt Saphronia said nothing but fixed a solemn, steady gaze on Mandie.

"Why Papoose alone?" the old man asked.

Mandie didn't really know where to begin. "Well . . ." she stalled, "you see . . . my mother has a new baby, and he cries and screams night and day, hardly ever stopping. I just can't stand the racket." Once Mandie started talking, the words tumbled out in a steady stream.

"Not only that," she continued, "my mother doesn't have any time for me anymore. That baby takes up every minute. Sometimes she doesn't even leave him so she can eat. And when I got home from school the other day, I found that Uncle John had gone to Richmond on business and left my mother to tend to that crying baby." Stopping to take a breath, she watched for the old Indians' reactions.

"Humph!" Uncle Wirt grunted loudly. "Papoose ask Mother to come here?"

"N-no, but I left her a note," Mandie said, lowering her eyes. "She'll know where I am when she finds the note. She's probably found it by now."

"Humph!" the old Indian said again. "Papoose know must ask Mother. Papoose must go home. Ask Mother."

"Uncle Wirt, please let me stay," Mandie begged. "You are my kinspeople."

Uncle Wirt shook his head. "Go home when sun come up," he insisted. "No more talk."

Mandie looked pleadingly at Aunt Saphronia, but the old woman just shook her head.

Uncle Wirt stood up. "Must send word. Cherokee powwow. Council house. School."

He quickly left the cabin, leaving Mandie and Aunt Saphronia sitting there. Mandie knew it was useless to argue anymore tonight, but tomorrow morning she would try again.

"Wash," Aunt Saphronia told her as she rose and pointed to the washbasin on the shelf by the back door. "Sleep."

Both words sounded good to Mandie. "I know. I'm absolutely filthy," she agreed. Walking across the room to the front door, she picked up her flour sack, which she had dropped when she came into the cabin. "I'll take water in the back room and clean up," she said.

"Yes," Aunt Saphronia nodded. She continued cleaning up the remains of their supper.

Mandie glanced over at the fireplace. Snowball still lay curled up there, snoozing away.

Uncle Wirt's house was larger than the other cabins at Bird-town. Behind the main room, there was a small room Uncle Wirt and his wife used for a bedroom. Most of the Cherokee cabins had only one large room that was curtained off for privacy at bedtime.

Mandie took a pan of clean water, a washcloth, soap, and towel, together with her flour sack, into the back bedroom to wash up and change into the only other dress she had with her. She had had only two dresses when she left Charley Gap to go live at Uncle John's house, and that was all she brought back here with her. She didn't want any of the fine clothes Uncle John had given her.

After bathing and dressing, Mandie brushed out her tangled hair. As she was plaiting it again into one long braid down her back, she heard voices in the main room.

What if her mother had found the note and sent someone here to look for her? What should she do? Give in? What would her mother do if she didn't?

Carrying the pan of water, she opened the door and went into the main room. Tsa'ni sat near the hearth, talking to his grandmother. Mandie angrily threw the water out the back door, then returned to confront her cousin.

Refreshed after washing and changing clothes, Mandie felt up to a serious conversation with Tsa'ni. Quietly walking across the room, she sat down on a small stool near him. He looked over at her with a sulky expression as his grandmother returned to the kitchen to wash the dishes.

"Tsa'ni, why did you tell me a lie?" she asked. "You said you weren't going to your grandfather's house. Yet when I finally got here, you were just about to take off in your wagon."

"I told you. I changed my mind," the Indian boy replied. "Besides, I do not have to give you a ride if I do not want to."

Mandie heard Aunt Saphronia gasp at his smart remark.

Tsa'ni stood up and stepped outside. Mandie followed. It was already dark, but the full moon shone brightly.

"No, you don't have to give me a ride, but you could at least tell the truth," Mandie said. "I'm not your enemy, Tsa'ni. I want to be your friend. We *are* cousins, in case you've forgotten."

Tsa'ni walked over to a long fallen log and sat down. Mandie joined him, sitting on the other end.

The Indian boy pulled a piece of wood and a knife

out of his pocket. "I do not claim to be cousins with a white girl," he said, beginning to whittle.

"You know I am one-fourth Cherokee," Mandie reminded him. "Your grandfather accepts me as his niece. Why can't you forget this hatred you have against white people? We are all what God made us, and there's nothing and nobody who can change that."

Tsa'ni whittled away on his wood. "Oh, but you are talking about your God," Tsa'ni returned sharply, without looking up.

Mandie wanted to ask what he meant by that, but just then Riley O'Neal wandered into the yard from the road. Instantly, Tsa'ni took off running without saying a word.

The missionary watched him go, then shrugged. "I trust you have recuperated from your journey now, Amanda," he said as they walked back to the house.

"Yes, thanks. I feel much better," she replied. "After all, I was pretty dirty." She laughed and smoothed the folds of her long skirt. "Did you go far on your walk?"

"I just went into the woods a little ways," he told her. "The woods have always fascinated me. All of God's little creatures hide in there, and you never know what you might find."

Hearing the sound of horses and a wagon, Mandie glanced behind them. "Here comes Uncle Wirt," she said. Mandie and the missionary walked toward for the barn where the old Indian took the wagon. As Uncle Wirt pulled in, they stepped inside the barn and the young missionary reached into his own rig for his valise.

As Uncle Wirt unharnessed the horses, he said, "Cherokee Powwow when sun at top of sky tomorrow."

Riley O'Neal looked puzzled.

"At noon tomorrow," Mandie explained. Then she turned to her uncle. "May I go, too, Uncle Wirt? Please?"

The old Indian shook his head. "Must go home when sun up," he replied, starting toward the house.

Mandie tried to catch up to his long strides. "Oh, Uncle Wirt, please let me go to the council house," she begged. "Besides, if all the Cherokees are at the powwow, who will take me home?"

"Humph!" was all the old Indian would say as he continued on to the house.

Mandie and Riley O'Neal followed him into the cabin.

Inside, Aunt Saphronia was sitting at the table, knitting some indigo blue yarn that lay on the table.

Mandie passed by her without saying anything. "Uncle Wirt, please let me go to the powwow tomorrow," she pleaded. "Please."

The old Indian turned. "Bed," he said sharply. "Time Papoose go to bed." He pointed to the ladder leading to the loft where she would sleep.

Knowing there was no point in arguing anymore that night, Mandie sighed, picked up her sleeping kitten, and headed up the ladder. "Good night everybody," she said sullenly. All she could do was try again in the morning.

Chapter 8 / "I Can't Go Home!"

For a long time Mandie lay awake on the cornshuck mattress in her loft sleeping quarters. Although she was worn out from her long journey, she was too wound up to sleep.

As the cool night air blew through the window and Snowball prowled around the tiny room, Mandie thought about home. In her mind she could hear the baby screaming. She could see her tired mother trying to hush him. Dr. Woodard had said her mother didn't have to tend the baby every minute, but she insisted on taking care of him all the time.

I hope Mother's sorry about neglecting me to spend so much time with that baby, she thought. Mandie loved her mother so much that she didn't want to share her with anyone else. *But,* she thought, *evidently Mother doesn't love me enough to spend time with me.*

Mandie wiped away a tear and rolled over on the cornshuck mattress. Somehow she would have to convince Uncle Wirt to let her stay. Otherwise, she would have to find somewhere else to go. *I'm not going back home,*

100

she cried to herself. *I'm not going where I'm not wanted.*

When Mandie finally drifted off to sleep, she was so upset and exhausted that she tossed and turned for a long time with horrible nightmares. Tsa'ni was chasing her down the mountain, and her mother was calling to her from somewhere in the woods.

Mandie rolled over onto the kitten, and he squirmed and meowed loudly in protest. Startled, Mandie woke and found the bright sunlight already streaming into the loft from the window.

"Oh, Snowball, it must be past breakfast time!" she cried, jumping up to look out the window. There was no one in sight. She swiftly pulled on her dress. Smelling the aroma of coffee, she grabbed the kitten and opened the door to her room. "Come on, let's go downstairs," she said.

Rushing down the ladder, she found Aunt Saphronia alone in the big room, still preparing the morning meal. Relieved that she hadn't missed breakfast, Mandie put Snowball down and offered to help.

The old woman smiled and shook her head. "No, no. Dishes on table. Food in pan. Men outside. Soon eat."

Mandie looked out through the open front door. Uncle Wirt and Riley O'Neal were standing near the road, talking.

As Mandie watched, another wagon came up the road and turned into the driveway. *Uncle Ned!* She shrank back inside the doorway. He would tell her mother she was here. *That's silly,* Mandie told herself. *Mother knows where I am. When I left the note that I was going to visit my Cherokee kinspeople, she knew that meant Uncle Wirt and Aunt Saphronia.*

But Mandie knew Uncle Ned wouldn't be happy with her for running away from home. She had promised to try to be happy with the baby. Now all she could do was wait for her old Indian friend to come in.

Suddenly she realized Uncle Ned wasn't alone. His granddaughter Sallie was with him.

Sallie jumped down from the wagon and straightened her full red skirt and white waist.

Mandie rushed out to meet her. "Sallie!" she cried, embracing her friend. "I'm so glad to see you."

Sallie smiled and returned the welcome. "I am glad to see you, too, Mandie." The shell necklace around her neck jingled.

Mandie noticed Uncle Ned talking to the other men. "Did my mother send your grandfather to find me?" she asked.

"I am afraid she did," Sallie told her. "Mandie, your mother is worried for you."

Mandie sighed and plopped down on the fallen log nearby.

Sallie sat down beside her. "Dr. Woodard is also looking for you," Sallie continued. "The hospital is ready. And he wants you to be there for the opening."

Mandie brightened. "It is? At last!" she exclaimed. "Oh, Sallie, that's wonderful!" She clasped her hands in delight.

"You should not be so happy when your mother is so worried," Sallie rebuked her gently.

Mandie calmed down and looked at her Indian friend. "I'm just happy about the hospital finally being finished," she explained. "I *am* sorry my mother is worried, but I left her a note."

"But, Mandie, that was a dangerous journey for you to make alone," Sallie scolded, shaking her finger at her friend. "Terrible things could have happened to you."

"But they didn't." Mandie refused to think about the close calls she had encountered.

"Your mother did not know that. Oh, Mandie, I am afraid you have been so foolish," Sallie accused. As she shook her head, her long black braids swished in the air.

"But, Sallie, I couldn't stand that baby crying all the time," Mandie told her, her eyes misting. "And my mother didn't have any time for me. I figured she wouldn't even miss me."

"Mandie!" Sallie gasped. "You know better than that! Your mother loves you so much. You are lucky to have her. I wish my mother were still living."

Mandie reached for Sallie's hand and held it tightly. "I know," she said on the verge of tears. "I love my mother, and I guess I know she loves me, but it just doesn't seem like it right now. She spends all her time with that noisy baby. Maybe I'll go back home when he's grown up and stops all that howling."

Mandie looked up to see Uncle Ned standing over her. The old Indian gave Sallie a little nudge so he could sit next to Mandie on the log. Sallie got up and went inside the house, where the men had just gone.

As Uncle Ned put his arm around Mandie's shoulder, she tried to speak, but nothing came out.

Uncle Ned looked directly at Mandie with sadness in his dark eyes. "Papoose bad," he told her bluntly. "Must go home to Mother."

Mandie tried to shrink back from him, but he held her firmly.

"I don't want to go home, Uncle Ned," she finally managed. "I want to stay here." Again she poured out her hurts and frustrations.

"Mother of Papoose send love, say please come home," the old Indian told her, watching her face closely.

Mandie looked up at him sadly. "Uncle Ned, I love you. I always will, but I can't go home."

Uncle Ned tried to convince her, but Mandie wouldn't give in. Finally the old Indian rose stiffly. "Then I go back. Tell mother of Papoose," he said.

Mandie's heart melted a little. "And would you tell her I'm just fine?" she asked.

The old Indian said nothing but held out his hand to her, and the two of them went inside for breakfast.

The subject of her returning home did not come up at the breakfast table. Mandie was surprised that Uncle Wirt didn't mention it. He was the one who had insisted she had to go home.

Mandie remained unusually quiet during the meal, and Sallie didn't say much either. The two girls listened quietly to the others' conversation, most of which centered around the forthcoming council meeting to make a decision about the missionary's school.

When breakfast was over, the men went outside and the girls helped Aunt Saphronia clean up the table. By the time Mandie and Sallie were free to go outside, the men had disappeared.

The girls sat on the fallen log talking for a while, and Mandie told her friend that she was not going to let Uncle Ned take her home.

Sallie shook her head. "Your uncle may say you have to go," she reminded her.

"I don't think he will," Mandie said. "He told me last night that I had to go this morning, and he hasn't even mentioned it. I believe he changed his mind."

"I would not be so sure about that," Sallie warned.

Just then a wagon pulled off the road into Uncle Wirt's driveway. The girls stood and shaded their eyes from the sun to see who it was.

"Dimar!" they exclaimed together, hurrying to meet him.

Their friend Dimar Walkingstick lived in the mountains. He was the one who had found the girls and Joe Woodard when they got lost one time. Today Dimar's mother, Jerusha, rode with him in the wagon.

Dimar was helping his mother down when he caught sight of Mandie and Sallie. His face lit up and he turned to greet them.

"Mandie! Sallie!" Dimar cried. "I am so glad you are here."

Mandie smiled at the handsome boy. "I'm glad to see you again, Dimar," she said. Then she turned to his mother and greeted her with an embrace.

After exchanging greetings with the girls, Jerusha smiled. "Nice day. See friends," she said. "Vote."

"Vote?" Mandie questioned. "Oh, I understand. Y'all came for the council meeting to vote on Mr. O'Neal's school."

They all walked toward the house.

"He looks young to be a preacher," Sallie remarked.

Mandie smiled again. "Yes, he does," she admitted, "but I don't suppose there's any age limit to be one."

As they entered the big log cabin, Jerusha exchanged greetings with Aunt Saphronia.

"Saphronia!" Jerusha exclaimed, sitting on the nearest bench. "This strange man stay with you?"

"Yes. Nice man," the old Indian woman replied as she sat down beside her guest. "Make good school."

The young people went outside again to talk. It had been quite a while since Dimar had seen Mandie, and now she noticed he couldn't take his eyes off her. He listened closely while she related the events of her journey to Uncle Wirt's house.

Although he didn't say anything, Mandie knew he disapproved of her running away from home. It seemed everybody thought she had done the wrong thing.

Soon another wagon pulled into the yard. This time it was Uncle Wirt's son, Jessan, and his wife, Meli—Tsa'ni's parents. And Mandie was delighted to see that they had also brought Morning Star, who was Uncle Ned's wife and Sallie's grandmother.

Mandie ran out to meet Morning Star. A big grin spread over the old woman's face when she saw Mandie, and she held the girl so close, Mandie could hardly breathe.

"Papoose!" Morning Star exclaimed. "Not lost!"

"No, I'm not lost," Mandie replied. The woman knew Uncle Ned had come ahead to look for her.

"Vote," Morning Star said as they walked toward the house.

"Yes, I know. You are here to vote," Mandie said. "Mr. O'Neal is a nice man, Morning Star. He could probably do a lot of good for the Cherokee people if y'all will let him build a school for you."

Sallie nodded. "Yes, my grandmother. He is a nice man," she agreed.

At that moment the missionary, Uncle Wirt, and Uncle Ned came in from walking in the fields behind the house. All the Indians stopped to stare at the red-haired newcomer in his black suit and hat.

There were greetings all around, and everyone entered the house. The missionary smiled and repeated each name as he was introduced. The Cherokees didn't return the smile, Mandie noticed. They were a shy people.

As the adults visited among themselves, Mandie and her friends gathered in a corner of the big room to talk about what they had been doing since they last saw each other.

When Mandie glanced over at Uncle Ned, she saw him talking to Uncle Wirt and looking at her every now and then. She knew they must be discussing her. She hoped Uncle Wirt had decided to let her stay at his house.

After a few minutes Riley O'Neal came over to speak to the young people. Mandie introduced everyone, and it wasn't long before they were all talking as if they were old friends.

When Mr. O'Neal mentioned the possible new school, Dimar looked at him uncertainly. "We have a good school in the next town, sir," he told the missionary.

"Yes, we do," Sallie agreed.

"But with the money my church has allotted, we could give you a much better school—right here," the missionary told them.

"And I think we could make it attractive enough so that all the young Cherokees would like to attend it. In fact, we can even teach the older people who have never gone to school," he said.

"Could you teach my grandmother to speak English?" Sallie asked.

"And my mother?" Dimar added. "Neither of them knows more than a few words of English."

The missionary smiled. "We could certainly try very hard," he promised. "We would need to hire one of your people who speaks both languages, first. Of course, we would pay them a salary, and we would pay other people to take care of the school, and to build it right in the first place," he said. "And when the students finish with this school, we will pay for their higher education at another school."

Sallie and Dimar looked at each other in disbelief. "You would?" they both asked together.

Mandie knew both her friends were anxious to get all the education they could.

"What would the students have to do to get higher education?" Sallie asked.

"As soon as they finished certain books and could pass certain examinations, we would transfer them to one of our many schools around the country," the young man explained.

"Around the country?" Mandie questioned. "You have schools in other places?"

"Oh, yes, we have schools all over the United States," the missionary replied.

"I would have to leave home, then, if I wanted to get a higher education?" Sallie asked.

Riley O'Neal smiled. "Yes," he said, "but you would be given a choice about where you wanted to go."

Dimar leaned forward. "Would it depend on what we planned to learn?" he asked.

"That's right," the missionary agreed. "If you wanted to be a doctor, say, you'd go to a different school than that of a person who wanted to be a lawyer or teacher or nurse or preacher."

Dimar nodded thoughtfully. "It sounds as though you have come to give us a great opportunity," he said.

"Yes," Sallie agreed.

As the time for the council meeting approached, the adults started gathering in the doorway, calling to each other about who would ride in which wagon.

Mandie laughed. "I think we'd better join the crowd or we may get left behind," she said.

Snowball had been running around everywhere all morning, and now he came up to his mistress as though he knew she was going somewhere.

"Snowball!" Sallie exclaimed, stooping to pick him up. "Where have you been?"

Mandie eyed her kitten with a grin. "I know where he's been. Wherever he can find food," she said, laughing.

Dimar reached out to rub the kitten's head. "Are you taking him with us to the council house?" he asked.

Mandie thought for a moment. "Do you think it'd be all right?"

"I think so," Sallie said. "If you leave him here, he may get lost."

"I'm not sure he'll behave during the meeting," Mandie said.

"We will help you watch him," Dimar promised.

A few minutes later the young people piled into Dimar's wagon and asked the missionary to join them. Riley O'Neal climbed onto the seat next to Dimar, and the girls and the kitten rode in the back. Dimar's mother went with Uncle Ned and Morning Star.

The young people asked around, but no one had seen

Tsa'ni. His parents were there, but he had not shown up. Yet just as Dimar pulled his wagon onto the road, Tsa'ni came running up behind them and jumped onto the back of the wagon, uninvited.

Looking around, he quickly moved away from Sallie, who was holding the white kitten. "That white cat!" he said with disgust. "Mandie, do you have to take it every place you go?"

"Yes, Tsa'ni," Mandie replied. "He does belong to me, you know."

"Are you going to let him vote, too?" Tsa'ni retorted.

The missionary turned around to look at the troublesome boy. "I heard them call you Tsa'ni," he said. "You must be Mr. Pindar's grandson."

"Yes, I am," Tsa'ni replied. "And you must be that new preacher that everyone is talking about."

"I am Riley O'Neal," the missionary introduced himself.

"I know your name," Tsa'ni said.

The other young people rode on in embarrassed silence. Mandie hoped the missionary didn't judge all Cherokees by Tsa'ni's rude behavior.

"I am glad to meet you, Tsa'ni," Riley O'Neal said with a smile.

Tsa'ni didn't seem to know how to respond to the missionary's kindness.

But Mandie knew Tsa'ni could make trouble at the council meeting. They might have a rough time at the powwow if her cousin decided to vote against the missionary's school, because he would be allowed to tell why he was against it. *Oh, why can't he accept white people?* she wondered.

Mandie quickly closed her eyes and said a silent prayer.

Chapter 9 / Powwow!

Several hundred Cherokees were milling around the council house, laughing and talking when they arrived. The young Indian girls, who looked as if they were wearing their best dresses, shyly chatted with the young Indian men.

Mandie had been there before, but she gazed excitedly at the seven-sided, dome-roofed structure, where so many important issues were settled.

As Dimar slowed the horses to look for a place to park the wagon, Tsa'ni suddenly jumped down without a single word and disappeared into the crowd.

"Well!" Mandie exclaimed.

Dimar pulled off to one side of the road under some trees. "I hope he does not cause trouble at the voting," he remarked.

"He'd better not!" Mandie declared.

Riley O'Neal turned to look at Mandie. "What seems to be his problem?"

Mandie laughed. "Oh, he has lots of problems," she said, "the main one being that he hates white people.

Even though I am one-fourth Cherokee and I am also his cousin, he considers me some kind of foreigner."

"Maybe we can help him if we can get our school started here," the missionary told her.

"We wish you would," Sallie sighed.

Dimar set the brake on the wagon. "Even his grandfather cannot control him," he said.

They all got down from the wagon and walked toward the council house, where Uncle Wirt was waiting in the doorway. Mandie stroked her white kitten as they approached the old Indian.

Uncle Wirt greeted the missionary with a firm handshake. "You say about school. You leave. We vote."

Riley O'Neal looked a little puzzled. "You want me to tell the people about the school, right?" he asked.

Uncle Wirt nodded.

"And then I am supposed to go outside while you vote, right?"

"Yes," the old Indian confirmed. "Come." He led the way into the council house, where almost all the benches were full. Stout log poles held up the dome-shaped thatched roof, and the symbols of the various clans adorned the posts. The place of the sacred fire lay directly ahead as they entered. Behind the fire sat six men with stacks of papers and books.

Uncle Wirt turned to the young people and motioned to a bench nearby. "Sit," he said. Then gesturing to the missionary, he said, "Come."

Mandie sat between Sallie and Dimar and watched Uncle Wirt lead the young man to the front row, where they both sat down.

Mandie looked around for Uncle Ned and the others

who left from Uncle Wirt's house. She spotted Aunt Saphronia sitting way over to her left, but she didn't see Uncle Ned or Tsa'ni. It was Tsa'ni who worried her.

"Where are Uncle Ned and Tsa'ni?" she whispered to her friends.

Sallie and Dimar looked around and shook their heads.

As the drums sounded from one corner of the council house, the man in the center of the group by the fire stood and spoke a few words in Cherokee. Mandie couldn't understand him. She looked at Dimar.

"He is asking your Uncle Wirt to introduce the missionary," Dimar told her in a whisper.

The man sat down and Uncle Wirt stood to face the crowd. Speaking a few words in Cherokee, he motioned to the missionary and said, "Tell. Go." He motioned to the platform in front of them.

Riley O'Neal got up, smiled at Uncle Wirt, and stepped up on the platform.

He told the people about his church in Boston, about their desire to build a school for the Cherokee people, and about the money they were prepared to give toward the project. The Indians stared at him in silence.

Mandie knew *some* of the Indians could understand him as he spoke in English, but many could not. She wondered why no one was translating as he spoke.

"Of course, it is up to you people to vote on this offer," he said with a smile. "And we hope you will accept our assistance. I thank you very much. God bless you all."

Even though many of the Indians didn't understand what he said, they politely applauded as he stepped down and walked to the side door of the council house.

Uncle Wirt stood and looked down at a man sitting on one of the front benches. He motioned for him to come forward. To Mandie's amazement, the man was her Uncle John! And as he got up, Mandie saw Uncle Ned beside him. *How did Uncle John get here, and when?* she wondered.

Uncle Wirt said something to Uncle John in Cherokee. Then Uncle John mounted the platform and began talking in the Cherokee language. Mandie glanced over at the side door. Riley O'Neal still stood there, watching.

"What is he saying?" Mandie whispered nervously to Dimar.

"He is roughly translating what the missionary just said and telling them the school would be a great opportunity for our people," Dimar whispered in reply.

Mandie's heart beat faster. She would soon have to face her uncle. In fact, she decided, he probably made the trip here just to take her home. She usually got her way with Uncle John, but she doubted if she would this time.

When her uncle finished speaking, he sat down and the people clapped and stomped their feet. Snowball clung to his mistress in fear of the noise.

The man in the center stood up once more and quieted the people. "Vote," he said.

The missionary started to leave, but just then there was a commotion at the back of the council house. Everyone turned to see Tsa'ni stomping up the aisle to the front.

"There will be no vote until I have had my say!" the angry Indian boy shouted.

Uncle John stood and took him by the arm. "Tsa'ni,

you may have your say, but at least be civilized about this," he said sternly.

Mandie's heart pounded. Somehow she had known this was going to happen.

"Civilized?" Tsa'ni mocked. He looked out at the roomful of Cherokees. "Did you hear that? The white people do not consider the Cherokees civilized. That is what that white preacher man is here for. He wants to *civilize* us."

Riley O'Neal rushed back to the platform, shaking his head. "No, Tsa'ni, that's not true," he said gently. "We want to teach the Cherokee people, train them for jobs so they can make a better living. Wouldn't you like for your people to advance in this world? With an education, they can. That's what we're here to do."

"You are only here to put our people down and teach that white men's ways are better than ours," Tsa'ni argued hotly.

A buzz of whispers swept through the crowd as those who understood the dispute in English translated for those nearby.

The missionary's face tensed, but his voice remained calm. "That is *not* our intent," he replied. "We only want to help. He turned to the rest of the Cherokees. "We hope you will give us that opportunity." He hurried out the side door.

Tsa'ni looked flustered. "We do not need your help!" he cried. "We are a proud people, are we not? Let the Cherokees decide," he said confidently. "I vote no!"

A hush fell over the room for a moment.

"Vote," the man in the center called out again.

Mandie's stomach felt like it was tied in knots. Would

her Cherokee kinspeople be swayed by Tsa'ni's angry appeal?

The audience got up and started filing by the front platform. The six men there gave out pieces of paper. The Cherokees scribbled on them and handed them back to the last man in the row.

Dimar stood. "Come on, Mandie," he said. "We will vote. All you have to do is write yes or no on the piece of paper."

Mandie and Sallie followed him in line. Mandie took her piece of paper and handed Snowball to Sallie while she quickly wrote the word *yes*. Then she gave the paper to the man in charge.

Taking Snowball back, Mandie waited for Sallie. The people milled around in the council house and some went outside after they voted. Mandie avoided looking in Uncle John's direction.

Dimar stood at the open doorway. "Let us wait outside," he suggested. "When they count the votes, they will let us know. I see the missionary out there."

The girls worked their way through the crowd and followed Dimar out the doorway. Riley O'Neal was sitting on a tree stump nearby in the shade. He held his black hat in his hands, and the wind blew through his curly red hair.

Dimar sat down on the ground beside him, and the girls joined him. "They will be counting the votes, and they will let us know the result soon," Dimar told the missionary.

Riley O'Neal fidgeted with his hat in his hands.

He looks nervous, Mandie thought.

"Do you think they understood that we only want

good for them?" the missionary asked Dimar.

"Not many of the Cherokees speak English," Dimar said, "but Mandie's uncle translated your speech very well. He is a very educated man."

"Is he also Cherokee?" Riley O'Neal twirled his hat.

Mandie spoke up. "He is one-half Cherokee," she said proudly. "You see, he is my father's brother, and their mother was Uncle Wirt's sister. After my father died, Uncle John married my mother." Her voice quavered slightly.

"Then he does not live here with the Cherokees?" the missionary asked.

"Oh, no. We live in Franklin," Mandie told him.

Suddenly the drums inside the council house sounded, and the beating grew louder and louder to an almost deafening roar.

Dimar motioned to the others, including Riley O'Neal, to return to the council house with him. Uncle Wirt met the missionary at the door and escorted him to the front, where the two of them sat with Uncle John and Uncle Ned. This time the young people sat on a bench at the back. The building filled quickly with Cherokees, and the drums stopped.

The man in the center stood.

Mandie held her breath as the man said something quickly in Cherokee. Then in English he said, "Vote, yes. We take school."

Mandie clapped and hugged her friends as the crowd again applauded and stomped their feet. With all the noise, Snowball huddled in a frightened little ball on Mandie's lap. She rubbed his head to comfort him.

Uncle Wirt motioned for the missionary to take the

platform. Riley O'Neal stood and held up his hand for silence.

The crowd immediately hushed.

With a big smile, the missionary nodded gratefully. "Thank you all. Thank you. We will begin to make plans immediately." Then he said something quietly to Uncle John on the front row.

John Shaw stood and looked around the council house. He said something in Cherokee, then changed to English. "May we have a word of prayer, please?" he asked.

There was complete silence as the crowd waited.

The missionary began a prayer in English, and after each sentence Uncle John translated it into Cherokee. The young man concluded with, "May the Lord bless you and keep you. Amen." The crowd stood and began talking excitedly with one another.

Mandie took a deep breath as she and her friends rose from their places. She saw Uncle John headed her way.

"I will take Snowball with me," Sallie said, taking the kitten from Mandie.

Dimar and Sallie disappeared into the crowd.

As soon as Uncle John reached Mandie, he put his arm around her shoulders and led her to a quiet spot outside. He looked deep into her blue eyes. "Amanda," he said with firm gentleness, "why did you run away?"

Tears sprang into her eyes, and Mandie looked down. "I . . . I just want to stay with my Cherokee kinspeople, Uncle John," she replied, trying to keep her voice steady.

"But you cannot stay here, Amanda," he told her. "Your mother is worried and upset about what you have done. Don't you love her?"

Mandie looked up at him quickly. "Of course, Uncle John. Next to my father I love my mother most," she answered. "But she doesn't love me anymore."

"Amanda, you know that is not true," Uncle John protested. "She loves you with all her heart."

"But she has to spend all her time tending to that new baby," Mandie began. "I—"

Uncle John beamed. "You can't imagine how proud I am of that little fellow."

Mandie knew she was treading on delicate ground. "But he yells all the time, all day and all night," she said bitterly.

"I know, but he will soon outgrow that," her uncle replied. Then with a smile he added jokingly, "Maybe he doesn't like the family he was born into."

Mandie hadn't thought about that. Maybe the baby didn't want her for a sister. It could work both ways. But then that was a silly idea, she thought. How could a new-born baby decide anything like that?

Uncle John's face sobered. "Let's go, Amanda," he said, taking her hand.

"Oh, please let me stay at Uncle Wirt's house," Mandie begged. "I don't want to go home. Besides, Sallie said the hospital is ready to be opened, and I have to be here for that. Please?" She looked up pleadingly into her uncle's face. He looked so much like her father even though he was fifteen years older.

"Yes, I know the hospital is finished," he said. "Dr. Woodard came by and told your mother while I was in Richmond. I got home late yesterday, and when I found out you had run away, I came on over to Bird-town. Your mother told me she had sent Uncle Ned, but I felt it was my place to come for you."

He looked at her and shook his head. "Amanda, it was so foolish of you to run away all alone like that through the mountains and woods and deserted roads. You could have been killed! It was just a blessing that the missionary came by and found you, rather than someone with bad intentions."

"I'm sorry that I caused you and Mother to worry about me," Mandie said. "But now that you know I'm all right, can't I stay?" she begged.

Uncle John hesitated a moment. "I am not excusing your running away, Amanda, but I know how important it is for you to be here for the hospital opening. I've decided to let you stay until then, but you will come home immediately after that," he said firmly.

Mandie buried her head in her uncle's chest and fought back tears. She couldn't promise him she would go home. *I can't!* she thought. *I have to find some way to stay here.*

Uncle John patted her back and Mandie looked up. "Now that we have all that settled," he said, "let's see where our friends are." He led Mandie through the crowd.

I'm glad he thinks it's settled, Mandie thought. *But I am not going home ever again!*

She winced at a stab of guilt, but she was determined to stay.

Uncle John led her over to Dimar's wagon. There they found Uncle Wirt, the missionary, Dimar, and Sallie trying to stay cool in the shade. The day had warmed up quickly.

As they approached, Mandie spoke to Uncle Wirt. "Uncle John has given me permission to stay at your house until the hospital opens," she said. "That is, if you don't mind having me."

Uncle Wirt reached out and put his arm around her. "Love Papoose. Now things right, you stay."

The old Indian didn't know much English and had trouble expressing himself sometimes, but Mandie appreciated his effort. She squeezed his big brown hand. "I love you, too, Uncle Wirt," she said. She took Snowball from Sallie and cuddled him.

Sallie and Dimar both smiled at her as other friends and relatives crowded around the missionary to talk. Everyone seemed curious about this stranger with curly red hair who had promised to build them a school, give them free books, and teach them free of charge.

Neither Mandie nor her friends had seen Tsa'ni anywhere until it was time to go back to Uncle Wirt's. Mandie was sure that he wasn't taking his defeat well.

But just as Dimar pulled his wagon away from the council-house grounds, Mandie's troublesome cousin hopped on and sat silently on the edge, away from everyone else. Then as they neared Uncle Wirt's driveway, he hopped off again and ran off down the road.

"Well! There he goes again!" Mandie exclaimed. She released Snowball, and he ran off to the Pindars' backyard.

Stopping in front of Uncle Wirt's house, Dimar turned to the missionary. "I wish Tsa'ni would behave better," he said.

The red-haired young man helped the girls out of the wagon. "We are used to dealing with boys like him," he assured him. "Maybe we can help Tsa'ni."

"I hope so," Sallie replied.

At that moment someone yanked Mandie's long blond braid from behind. Mandie whirled to see her friend

Joe Woodard grinning broadly.

"Joe!" she gasped. "When did you get here?"

"My father and I have been waiting in the house for you," the lanky boy explained.

Mandie looked around the yard. "But where is your buggy?" she asked.

"Behind the house," Joe said with a laugh.

"You hid it so you could surprise us!" Mandie laughed.

After the young people had all exchanged greetings, they walked over to the fallen log to sit down. As more adults drove up in their wagons, the missionary joined them inside.

Mandie looked over at her lifelong friend from Charley Gap, still not believing he had come. "How long are you going to stay, Joe?" she asked excitedly.

"Until they open the hospital," he replied, brushing his brown hair out of his eyes. "That's why my father is here." Then with a sly look, he asked, "How long are you staying?"

Obviously Joe knew she had run away from home. "Uncle John just told me I could stay until the hospital opens," she replied, trying to hide her embarrassment.

Before long Aunt Saphronia came to the doorway and called to them. "Come. Eat. Now," she said.

When it came to eating, Joe never had to be called twice. He jumped up and led the way.

At the dinner table, Uncle John sat next to Mandie, and in the course of the meal, he talked to her about his plans. "Dr. Woodard says the opening of the hospital is set for tomorrow, but I won't be able to stay for it. I must get home to your mother and the baby. I've been gone far too much already," he said. "So I will be leaving right after this meal. You may stay for the opening, but come home immediately afterward," he said again. "Uncle Ned has promised to bring you home. He had plans to travel in our direction anyway."

Mandie looked up at him, but said nothing. She was determined that she was not going home right after the ceremony, but she wasn't about to tell him that.

After dinner, as Uncle John was about to leave, he called to her from his rig. "By the way," he said, "I just remembered. Your mother sent you some clothes. I gave them to Aunt Saphronia. Have a good time. I'll be expecting you to leave as soon as the opening ceremony is over."

Mandie waved goodbye as he drove out the driveway onto the road and disappeared around the curve.

Then she turned to her friends. "Well, at least I'll have some clean clothes to wear to the hospital opening tomorrow," she said as they walked back into the cabin. "Did you bring extra clothes, Sallie?"

"Yes, I always bring spare clothes because I never know where I will be going when I leave with my grandfather," the Indian girl answered.

Joe and Dimar waited outside in the yard for them.

Inside, Aunt Saphronia picked up a valise and handed it to Mandie. "Clothes," she said.

"Thank you," Mandie replied. Taking the valise, she turned to Sallie. "Come on. Let's take this upstairs and see what my mother sent."

Up in Mandie's small loft room, she unpacked the neatly folded clothes. Then as she looked through them, she found a letter addressed to her.

Turning the envelope over in her hand, she frowned.

"This is a letter from my grandmother. I wonder why she is writing to me. Uncle John didn't say anything about it."

Sallie smiled and sat down on the corn-shuck mattress.

Mandie quickly put the clothes back into the valise and sat beside her friend to open the letter.

What would her grandmother have to say?

Chapter 10 / Surprise for the Hospital Opening

Mandie ripped open the envelope and pulled out the letter. It was only one page, but it was important. She read it silently.

Dear Amanda,

There is so little time before we are to leave for Europe in July, and I am concerned about what I am hearing from your mother. Elizabeth has told me that if you don't mend your ways, she will not allow you to make the trip. I must remind you that if you have to stay home, you will disappoint your friend Celia Hamilton. And I'm afraid it would cost me a lot of money, time, and trouble to cancel everything. Please think this over, Amanda. Remember, your actions affect more people than yourself.

Lovingly,
Grandmother

Sallie sat quietly while Mandie read, then Mandie quickly folded the sheet of paper and inserted it in the envelope.

"Is it bad news, Mandie?" Sallie asked.

"N-no, not exactly," Mandie said. She got up and

walked over to the window to look out.

She couldn't go to Europe unless she went home, and she didn't want to go home. She hated to ruin the trip for her friend and her grandmother, but what could she do? If she were going to live with the Cherokees and claim them for her kinspeople, she couldn't go running off to Europe. She felt caught in the middle.

As she stared out the window, she saw Joe and Dimar kicking some rocks in the driveway. "Come on, Sallie," she said, brushing her troubles aside. "The boys look bored down there waiting for us."

Scurrying down the ladder, the girls hurried out to the yard where their friends were discussing Tsa'ni.

Sallie sat down on a nearby tree stump. "He is a strange boy," she admitted. "But I have been thinking about the way he acts. I believe he is lonely and does not know how to make friends."

Joe and Dimar chuckled.

"I'll say he doesn't know how to make friends," Joe said. "And I don't think he's interested in learning."

Dimar nodded. "He may be lonely, but he also has a mean streak in him."

"I've tried lots of times to be friends with him," Mandie agreed, "but he just keeps being mean."

"Maybe he has not been taught how to love," Sallie suggested. "Loving is sharing, giving, and doing good things for other people. But Tsa'ni has not learned that yet."

"Maybe Mr. O'Neal *can* help him," Mandie suggested.

"I hope so—" Dimar agreed.

"Speaking of the missionary," Joe cut in, "he told me he would be going back to Boston after the hospital opening so he can make plans for the school here."

"When is he coming back?" Mandie asked. "I'd like to help with the school if there is anything I can do."

"I would, too," Sallie said.

"So would I," Dimar added. "I think it will be a good thing for our people."

"I suppose I'll have to help, too," Joe said, laughing. "I have no idea how, but there must be something all of us can do."

"Let's go on back to the house find Mr. O'Neal and tell him we all want to help," Mandie suggested, getting up and brushing off her skirt.

When they checked inside, Aunt Saphronia told them that some of the men were visiting out back. The young people found the missionary, Dr. Woodard, Uncle Ned, and Uncle Wirt sitting under the huge chestnut tree behind the cabin. As the young people approached, the men were discussing the hospital.

Mandie and her friends waited politely for a break in the conversation.

"Yes," Riley O'Neal was saying, "I thought that I wanted to be a doctor before I decided to become a missionary. I had a little medical training, so if there's anything I can do . . ."

The men looked up at the young people.

Mandie took a deep breath. "Mr. O'Neal, we've come to offer our help on the school," she told him. "All of us."

The missionary smiled. "Thank you all. I can use all the help I can get. When I return from Boston, we'll have a meeting and assign duties, and so forth. God bless you."

Dr. Woodard cleared his throat. "I believe we need to

have a meeting right now concerning the hospital opening," the doctor told them.

The young people sat down on the grass and listened.

Dr. Woodard took charge. "This will be a great surprise for you, Amanda, but a messenger brought word a
little while ago that the President of the United States is
sending his personal assistant, Mr. Adam Adamson, for
the ceremony, and—"

Mandie jumped up and down. "President McKinley is
sending Mr. Adamson?" she cried. "Oh, how wonderful!
Y'all remember him, Sallie, Joe?"

The two nodded.

"Dimar, wait till you meet this man!" Mandie cried.
"He is so nice!"

Dimar turned to Sallie. "I remember you told me
about him, Sallie, after you got back from Washington,"
he said. "It will be a great honor to meet the President's
personal assistant."

Dr. Woodard spoke again. "Mr. Adamson will arrive
early in the morning," he continued. "Uncle Ned has arranged for some young Cherokee men to meet him at
the train. All of us will have to be ready to go to the
hospital when he gets here."

Mandie was so excited she didn't hear all the plans.
She was remembering her recent journey to the White
House to visit President McKinley. That had been the
most exciting thing that had ever happened to her.

The day passed, full of talk about plans for the forthcoming ceremony. Since Mandie was in charge of the
gold that built the hospital, she would be one of the people on the platform with Dr. Woodard and Mr. Adamson.
And since Joe and Sallie helped find the gold, they would
be there, too.

The next morning they were all up by the time the roosters crowed, and Dimar appeared on the doorstep a few minutes later. He and his mother had spent the night with her sister, who lived nearby.

Mandie was so excited she could hardly eat a bite of breakfast. But even excitement couldn't ruin Joe's appetite. He heaped his plate three times with grits, sausage, eggs, pancakes, syrup, gravy, and hot biscuits, along with some fresh sliced tomatoes.

When Mandie saw all that he was eating, she gasped. "Joe Woodard, you're going to pop!" she exclaimed.

"I never gain an ounce, so I don't think I'll expand enough to pop," Joe replied, shifting his long lanky frame.

Sallie smiled. "Just wait until you are grown. Then all this food will make you widen."

At the sound of horses and wagons in the yard, everyone stopped eating to listen. They looked out the open doorway. Mandie spotted her friend, Adam Adamson, with the two Indian braves Uncle Ned had sent to bring him.

"Our company has arrived!" she exclaimed excitedly, excusing herself from the table.

Most of them were finished eating anyway, so they all crowded into the doorway to welcome the man from the President's house.

As the man alighted from the wagon, Uncle Ned, who had also met the man in Washington, stepped down the front steps to shake his hand. "Welcome, Mr. Adam," he said.

"Thank you, Mr. Sweetwater. I am very honored to be here," Mr. Adamson replied.

Mandie got a glimpse of him through the crowd and

noticed that he was not wearing the formal clothes she had always seen on him. He wore what looked like a homemade shirt and cotton breeches held up by a pair of bright red suspenders.

Mandie guessed that he had dressed that way in order to be accepted by the Cherokees. *What a smart politician,* she thought.

Uncle Ned led the President's assistant to Uncle Wirt nearby. "Mr. Adam, this Mr. Pindar," he said.

Uncle Wirt shook hands with Mr. Adamson. "Come. My house. Coffee," he said.

The curious crowd stared as the three men passed through into the house. At the doorway inside, Mr. Adamson spotted Mandie, Sallie and Joe. "Amanda," he said, putting his arm around her. "The President sends all of you young people his best wishes for a successful hospital operation."

Mandie, eager to introduce Dimar, spoke up. "Mr. Adamson, this is one of our very best friends, Dimar Walkingstick," she said.

Dimar stepped forward and shook hands with the President's assistant. "I am very honored to meet you, sir," he said.

"Any friend of these young people is a friend of mine," Mr. Adamson said with a smile.

As they walked farther into the room, Mandie introduced Mr. Adamson to the missionary. "Mr. O'Neal has come all the way from Boston to set up a school for the Cherokee people," she said proudly.

The men exchanged greetings.

As Uncle Ned steered Mr. Adamson toward the table, Aunt Saphronia brought a pot of hot coffee and set it on a plate on the table. She already had clean cups waiting.

When Mr. Adamson saw the tiny woman, he greeted her warmly. "Evidently you are the lady of the house, so you must be Mrs. Pindar," he said. "It's such a pleasure to meet you."

Aunt Saphronia understood more English than she could speak. A look of frustration crossed her face; then she said something rapidly in Cherokee and turned to Sallie to translate.

"She welcomes you to her house," Sallie told Mr. Adamson. "She is honored to have an emissary of the President of the United States visit the Eastern Band of Cherokees and drink her coffee."

Mr. Adamson took the old woman's hand and kissed it gallantly. "The pleasure is all mine, Mrs. Pindar."

Evidently Aunt Saphronia had never seen a woman's hand kissed before. Quickly withdrawing, she looked at her hand and then at Mr. Adamson. Then she smiled and said, "Sit."

As the men sat down at the table for coffee, Mandie looked at her simple blue calico dress and at Sallie's skirt and waist and Joe's everyday clothes. *Mr. Adamson is seeing us as we really are now,* she thought. *In Washington we had to dress up in all that finery and act like rich people. Today we can be ourselves.*

By the time they had all finished their coffee, the group had grown so large it covered the entire yard outside. The Cherokees had all come to look at the man from the President's house. Even though Uncle Ned told them to go ahead to the hospital, no one left. So when everyone was ready to go, almost all the Cherokees who lived in that area were lined up down the road.

The hospital had been built between Bird-town, where Uncle Wirt lived, and Deep Creek, where Uncle Ned lived. The caravan had to go to the Tuckasegee River and follow the road along the river for a while before cutting away into the woods.

Mandie and her friends rode in Uncle Ned's wagon, and Dimar's mother drove theirs. Mandie held Snowball on her lap and eagerly watched the road for her first glimpse of the hospital. The last time she saw the structure, someone had been tearing down the walls. It seemed the hospital would never be completed. The culprits had been caught, however, and now the building was finished. Mandie couldn't wait to see it.

Mr. Adamson sat on the seat with Uncle Ned, and they all discussed their Washington visit. Dimar listened with great interest.

"The President says that you all must visit him again soon," Mr. Adamson told them. "And perhaps you could come next time, Dimar."

Dimar glowed with happiness. "Thank you, Mr. Adamson. I would be honored to visit with the President."

Suddenly a flash of white through the trees caught Mandie's eye. "Here it is!" she cried excitedly. She bent forward, admiring the white frame structure with a small porch and two simple columns adorning the front. "Oh, Uncle Ned, it's beautiful!" she exclaimed.

The old Indian looked back at Mandie and then ahead to the hospital. "Yes. Good," he agreed.

After he pulled his wagon into the shade under the trees, the young people scrambled to the ground.

Mandie led the way, clutching her kitten. "Let's explore the inside of the hospital," she suggested. Then she saw the blue ribbon tied across the entrance.

"Oh, Mandie," Joe said, "you know my father arranged all this. The ribbon has to be cut before the doors are opened."

Mandie was disappointed. "I should have remembered," she said. "I knew it was going to be a formal ceremony with all the trappings, but I thought if we slipped up here ahead of time, we could go inside to look."

Sallie put her hand on Mandie's shoulder. "But that would spoil the surprise," she said.

"The surprise?" Mandie asked.

"Yes, the Cherokee people are all going to be surprised at how efficient and beautiful it is inside," Sallie replied. "You see, only a few of us worked on the furnishings. The others have no idea what is in there."

"Well, I don't either," Mandie said. "What is inside?"

Joe laughed. "Wait and see," he told her.

Mandie stroked her kitten and stared at the hospital for a moment. There were rooms jutting out of either side of the porch to protect the front door from the weather. Several chairs sat on the porch, and in the center a huge basket full of brightly colored flowers rested on a small table.

As the time for the ceremony approached, hundreds and hundreds of Cherokees piled out of wagons parked in a jumbled confusion beyond the hospital, out of sight. Everyone hurried toward the hospital, looking for a good place to view the proceedings. Benches had been provided for the old people, but the others had to stand.

Dr. Woodard took charge and directed certain people to the chairs on the porch. "Amanda, in the center chair, please," he called to her. "Joe, you sit on one side of her and Sallie on the other. Uncle Ned, Uncle Wirt, and Aunt Saphronia, sit here please." He indicated the chairs on the other side of the porch. "Mr. Adamson, would you please sit by the table there?"

Those he called hurriedly took their places. The young people scanned the crowd, whispering to each other as they spotted various people they knew.

Dr. Woodard tapped on the table to hush the noisy crowd milling around the building. "Ladies and gentlemen," he began.

There was complete silence as the crowd waited to see what was going to happen next.

"We would like to ask Uncle Ned Sweetwater to open our ceremony with a prayer," the doctor continued. "He has been instrumental in achieving this miracle we are looking at today. Without him this hospital would not have been. And we would ask that his granddaughter, Sallie Sweetwater, translate the prayer into English for us."

Dr. Woodard paused for a moment and cleared his throat. "And since I don't know the Indian language, I have also asked her to translate the rest of the ceremony into Cherokee for her people."

The doctor stepped aside and motioned for Uncle Ned to take his place in the center for the prayer. Sallie stood by his side as the old Indian lifted his black eyes toward the sky and began to pray in a loud voice. Since the Cherokee language is spoken in a very fast fashion, Sallie had to speed up her English translation to keep up with him.

There was a great response from the crowd. Some echoed Uncle Ned's words and others called out praises to God, but it all ended with a loud amen.

After Uncle Ned was seated, Dr. Woodard stepped back to the center of the porch. "And now, the President of the United States, William McKinley, has sent us a message, and his personal assistant, Mr. Adam Adamson, will deliver that message to us at this time. Mr. Adamson?"

As Sallie translated for Dr. Woodard, the man from the White House rose and began his speech. "President McKinley sends his love, first of all," he said.

The crowd burst into applause at the familiar English word *love,* even before Sallie translated it.

Mr. Adamson waited for the noise to subside, then continued. "The President regrets that he cannot be here for this occasion, but he has sent his message by me." He took a deep breath and smiled to the large crowd. "This is a great day for the Cherokee people. You now have your own hospital. And you also have one of the best doctors in this part of the country running it—the Cherokees' friend, Dr. Woodard."

Again the crowd applauded enthusiastically.

Mandie stroked her kitten in her lap. She was glad everyone was so excited. *But,* she thought, *if they keep interrupting like this, we'll never get finished and get inside.*

Mr. Adamson didn't talk much longer, and when he finished, the Cherokees applauded and stomped their feet.

Then it was Mandie's turn to speak. Even though she knew most of the people and a lot of them were her distant relatives, her palms were sweaty. She handed Snowball to Joe, who took the kitten reluctantly.

Mandie's voice trembled a bit at first, and she fidgeted

with her locket. "I love you, my Cherokee people," she began, trying to brush away any thoughts of home, Europe, or the baby.

Again the Cherokees responded to the word *love,* and she had a hard time quieting them. "I thank you for your confidence and trust in me when you gave me the gold that belonged to you."

Her voice grew stronger as she got caught up in what she was saying. "We have tried to spend it on the Cherokee people by building this beautiful hospital for our people. Dr. Woodard will be here at certain times of the month, and he is training some of our people to operate the hospital. Now you won't have to go all the way into town when you get sick or hurt."

She continued by thanking the people who actually built the structure. Then she insisted that Joe and Sallie be recognized for their part in finding the gold. Finally, she praised Dr. Woodard for his untiring supervision in building the hospital and in furnishing the interior with all the necessary equipment and furniture.

When she sat down, the applause was deafening, and some of the Cherokees stepped forward to give her a hug. Mandie took Snowball from Joe, feeling a little embarrassed at all the attention.

Dr. Woodard finally hushed the crowd by announcing that the ribbon cutting would now take place. After that the doors would be opened and the crowd could go inside to inspect the interior. The Cherokees listened intently as Sallie translated the proceedings.

"Of course the ribbon should be cut by the person who began this venture, Amanda Shaw," the doctor said. He turned and held out a large pair of scissors to her.

As she rose, Mandie's heart pounded. "Thank you, Dr. Woodard," she said, "but I cannot do that because the ribbon should be cut by one of the people who now owns it. And I know of no one better qualified than dear Uncle Ned Sweetwater."

She motioned to him, but he shook his head.

Mandie continued in a firm, low voice. "You are always taking care of me, Uncle Ned," she said, looking into his caring, dark eyes. "Now it's your turn to be honored. This hospital will not be opened until you cut the ribbon." She smiled at him.

Dr. Woodard offered the old man the scissors.

Uncle Ned smiled at Mandie and took them. Standing, he walked over to the bright blue ribbon across the doorway. Then turning to the people, he said something loudly in Cherokee.

Sallie translated into English. "We dedicate this hospital in the name of our great God and ask His blessings on it and on all who require its services." He closed the scissors on the ribbon.

As the bright blue ribbon fell into two pieces, Dr. Woodard flung open the front door and called to the already advancing crowd. "Please be careful of the furnishings and the floor," he cried. "So many people at once could possibly do damage. It is your hospital now. It's up to you to take care of it."

Mandie, Sallie, and Joe waited for Dimar to make his way through the crowd, and then they entered the hospital together.

Inside, Mandie gasped at the frilly yellow curtains and matching bedspreads on the six single beds in the spacious room. "Oh, Sallie, I see what you mean about a surprise!" she exclaimed. "You made these spreads and curtains, didn't you?"

Sallie nodded. "With the help of my grandmother and your Aunt Saphronia," she replied.

As the young people wandered around the hospital, the crowd gradually returned to their wagons and left. The young Indian men who had brought Adamson from the depot took him back after goodbyes and promises from the young people to come visit the White House again.

Uncle Wirt and Aunt Saphronia took Uncle Ned, Morning Star, and Dimar's mother, Jerusha, home with them after announcing that dinner would soon be on the table. Dr. Woodard and Riley O'Neal promised to see that Mandie, Joe, Dimar, and Sallie left with them shortly.

The doctor showed them details around the hospital that had been impossible to do with all the Cherokees milling around. He opened a cabinet in the small room reserved for an office and said, "This is where all the medical supplies are kept. I believe we have a good stock to start off with."

The others surveyed the rows of bottles, stacks of bandages, medical instruments and miscellaneous items on the shelves.

As Mandie opened her mouth to ask a question, there was a loud noise outside the window in the room which was on the front side of the hospital.

Rushing up to the glass pane to look outside, Mandie exclaimed, "It's Mr. Jason! And he has a young Indian man with him!"

"Mr. Bond!" Dr. Woodard puzzled. "Why, I wonder what he's doing all the way over here."

"Something must be terribly wrong!" Mandie cried and started for the door.

Chapter 11 / Trouble!

Flinging the front door open, Jason Bond rushed into the front hallway. Everyone crowded into the doorway of the office.

"Dr. Woodard, Miz 'Lizbeth sent me for you. She said to please come at once," Jason Bond hurriedly explained his mission.

Mandie quickly asked, "Where is Uncle John? Didn't he come home?"

"Missy, when I met him on my way to get the doctor he was hurrying on home," Mr. Bond explained, quickly. "Dr. Woodard, we can't waste any time."

"What's wrong, Mr. Bond?" the old doctor asked, as he grabbed his medical bag from a nearby table.

"The baby—something terrible is wrong with him. He can't breathe," Jason Bond explained.

"Help me unhitch my horse from the buggy. I can make better time on horseback," the doctor told Mr. Bond.

Mandie's heart pounded. She felt it must somehow be her fault. She had acted so horribly about the baby. In her mind she saw herself leaning over the cradle, saying, "You stupid baby! I wish you'd never been born!"

As the others rushed outside to help with the horse Mandie panicked. Overcome with guilt, she slipped away unnoticed and hurried out the back door of the hospital. Snowball had been wandering around inside, but Mandie didn't even think about him now. Hot tears blurred her vision, but she just kept running. She didn't even know where she was going. She just knew she had to get out of there.

She couldn't go home. The baby was probably dying, and it was all her fault. Her mother and Uncle John would hate her, she thought. Mandie couldn't go back to Uncle Wirt's house. He would make her go home. She would just have to find somewhere else to go. Nobody would want her now.

Heading for the woods, she ran and ran, stumbling over rocks that her tear-filled eyes couldn't see. Finally, when she could run no more, she fell exhausted on the ground and just lay there, sobbing.

A little while later, she felt something rub against her leg. She sat up quickly and looked around.

Her white kitten was batting something around with her paws. "Snowball!" she cried. She didn't pay any attention to what he was doing. He was always playing with a small rock or stick or acorn. Picking him up, she cuddled him against her chin. "Oh, Snowball, I'm so glad you found me. I couldn't go off without you. But we've got to get out of here."

As she stood, she shivered. The air felt chilly. She glanced up at the dark clouds rolling in. She didn't want to think about what that meant. "We've just got to get out of here," she repeated.

Holding Snowball tightly, she began running again. The more she thought about her predicament, the more worried she became. Tears filled her eyes. What was she going to do? Where was she going? She didn't know.

Light raindrops began to fall, and that only made Mandie cry all the harder. Pushing her way through thick bushes, she ran on blindly. The rain became heavier, drenching her clothes and making it more difficult to run. As she jumped over a huge fallen log, she stopped short and looked down.

A bear trap! She cringed. *I almost stepped right in it!* Her heart beat wildly as she remembered her close call with the bear on her way to Uncle Wirt's. This time she had no food to distract an attack. What would she do if she came upon another one?

As tears mingled with rain on her cold, wet face, she sat down on the log and cried out toward heaven. "Oh, dear God, I've been so awful. Grandmother is right. I've only been thinking of myself. Please help me know what to do." She stood and stroked her sopping wet kitten to comfort herself as much as her pet, and hurried on.

Suddenly a bolt of lightning struck a tree just off to the right. Mandie jumped. "Oh, dear God, please help!" she cried again. "Maybe I should go back. I'm scared to, but I don't know what else to do."

She glanced around her. All at once she realized that she didn't have any idea where she might be. Was she closer to the hospital or to Uncle Wirt's? Deafening thunder rumbled overhead. Mandie jumped, then looked up. The sky seemed almost black. She couldn't tell which direction to take for either place.

The cold rain poured down, and another flash of lightning struck nearby. Mandie sobbed uncontrollably and started running again. "Oh, Snowball, what are we going to do?" she cried. Rough branches caught her sopping clothes and tore at her skin as her feet slipped and slid in the mud beneath her. Snowball dug his claws into her shoulder in fright.

Then it happened! Her feet slipped and slid as she ran into a fallen log.

"Oh! Owww! Ohhh, no!" Mandie cried, falling to the ground in tremendous pain. She dropped Snowball, and he scampered away into the bushes. "No, Snowball!" she yelled. "Don't run away and leave me, here!" She looked down at her throbbing right leg. It was bleeding. "I'm hurt, Snowball. Really hurt!" she shouted. "Ohhh, please don't leave me here all alone!"

But Snowball was nowhere to be seen, and all Mandie could hear was the rumbling of thunder overhead and the steady drumming of the pouring rain. She tried to stand and instantly fell down again. "Oh, my leg is broken!" she cried.

Mandie groaned and tears streamed down her face as she writhed in agony. But any little movement made it far worse. Mandie grabbed the back of her neck and bit her lip, trying to brace herself against the pain.

Suddenly she realized her locket was gone! She had worn it to the hospital ceremony and now it was gone! It must have come off somewhere as she ran through the woods. Mandie wept all the louder, realizing the only picture she had of her dear father was lost with that locket forever.

Then she remembered how Snowball had been batting something around when he found her lying on the ground. "Oh, no!" she cried. "My locket probably came off when I fell there. I'll never be able to find that spot again!"

Mandie cried and cried as the pain in her leg only grew worse. The lightning flashed all around her, the thunder roared, and the rain poured harder and harder.

All of a sudden she heard noises in the bushes. *Bear!* she thought instantly, *And I can't walk! I don't have any way to escape!* She closed her eyes in terror.

"Papoose! Papoose!" someone called through the bushes.

Mandie recognized the voice. "Uncle Ned!" she called back with relief. "Uncle Ned, I'm over here. I'm hurt! Please help me!" she cried, trying to raise herself up.

The bushes in front of her parted, and out stepped the old Indian, drenched and worried-looking. Snowball bounded alongside him.

"Oh, Uncle Ned, I'm so glad to see you!" Mandie cried, wincing with pain. "How did you find me?"

"Doctor son come to house of Wirt. Say he not find Papoose," the old man explained, stooping to look at Mandie's leg. "I follow white kitten."

"It hurts so bad," she whispered. "Where's everybody else?"

"Doctor go see new papoose," Uncle Ned replied, frowning as he looked at the bleeding leg. "Others wait at hospital."

"Uncle Ned, I'm so sorry I've caused so much trouble," Mandie cried, trying not to pull away from the gentle hands on her leg that was causing her so much pain. "Oh-h-h-h!"

The old Indian grunted, stood up and quickly removed his deerskin jacket. He took off his shirt and put the jacket back on. He ripped the shirt into strips and tied them around Mandie's injured leg while she gritted her teeth in pain.

"Me go hospital," he told her, bending to pick her up. Then he remembered something and put his hand in his jacket pocket and withdrew Mandie's locket and gave it to her. "Papoose belong this."

"My locket!" Mandie gasped as she took it and held it tightly. "You found it! Thank you, Uncle Ned."

"Now we go hospital," Uncle Ned said, bending again and carefully picking Mandie up in his strong arms.

The old Indian began the long trek to the hospital, letting Snowball tag along behind. With his mistress hurt, the kitten probably wouldn't run off again.

As Uncle Ned trudged through the bushes carrying the injured girl, Mandie was in too much pain to try to talk, and she noticed that the old Indian was unusually silent.

Then he asked, "Why Papoose run away from hospital?" He looked down at her closely.

"I just don't know, Uncle Ned," Mandie said, sobbing. "I was scared. It was my fault the baby got sick."

Uncle Ned frowned and asked, "What Papoose mean?"

"I said something awful to the baby because I was so mad at the way he was screaming all the time," she admitted sheepishly.

Uncle Ned looked sharply at her. "Talk not make new papoose sick," he told her as he carefully stepped over a log in his path.

"But I have been mean about the baby, Uncle Ned. I

realize that now," she said, catching her breath in pain as her leg touched a big bush on the way. "I am really and truly sorry, Uncle Ned, for being mean to you, and to Mother, and to Uncle John, and most of all to the baby."

"Papoose always remember. Love. Think," the old man admonished her. As they reached the edge of the woods, the old man stopped and added, "Papoose must ask Big God forgive."

With one arm tightly around the old Indian's neck, she put her other hand over his wrinkled one holding her and squeezed it tightly. Mandie looked toward the cloudy sky that was now clearing in places and asked, "Dear God, will you please forgive me. I'm sorry I've been so mean. And, dear Lord, please don't let my little brother die. Please make him well. Please. Thank you."

Uncle Ned added to her prayer, "Yes, Big God, please make new papoose well. And please make Papoose's leg well. Thank you."

Mandie squeezed his hand again as he started on and said, "Uncle Ned, please forgive me."

"Big God forgive, I forgive," he told her.

Mandie smiled through her pain. Uncle Ned meant an awful lot to her.

After what seemed like hours, Uncle Ned carried Mandie out of the woods and stepped onto the lawn of the new Cherokee hospital. The rain had stopped and Riley O'Neal and Mandie's other friends hurried out to meet them.

"Mandie, are you all right?" everyone asked at once.

Riley O'Neal glanced at the makeshift bandages on Mandie's leg and then looked at her with concern.

Joe looked worried. "Too bad my father has left," he

said. "What are we going to do now?"

Riley O'Neal took charge, "Well, it looks to me as though Miss Amanda Shaw, the originator of this whole hospital project, is going to be its first patient. Let's get her inside."

Dimar and Joe looked at him and then at each other.

"Well, come on, boys. Let's help Uncle Ned get her inside," the missionary said, holding open the front door. "I can take care of this. I have had a little medical training."

Sallie hovered nearby as Uncle Ned brought Mandie through the doorway. She ran ahead and pulled down the frilly yellow bedspread on one of the beds. The old Indian laid Mandie on the clean, white sheets.

Mandie groaned with pain from the slight jolt. "I'm sorry, everybody," she said weakly.

"Do not worry, Mandie," Sally assured her, picking up Snowball. "We all love you and we will make sure this missionary takes good care of you."

Mandie faintly smiled, looking up at the missionary. "I guess if Dr. Woodard can't be here, you'll have to fix me up," she said, still clutching her locket.

Riley O'Neal bent over to examine her leg and winked at her as he smiled.

Chapter 12 / The Baby's Name Is ...

With Uncle Ned overseeing and Joe, Dimar, and Sallie to find the supplies he needed, it didn't take Riley O'Neal long to clean the wound. After a thorough examination he announced with a sigh of relief, "No bones broken, but it's an awfully bad sprained ankle."

He wrapped it as Mandie breathed deeply and said, "Oh, thank you, God."

"With some blankets in the wagon, you'll be all right to go on back to your uncle's house," the missionary told her. "We'll step outside and let you rest a few minutes first."

Mandie felt relieved. Now, more than anything else, she wanted to go home. She was still a little worried about what her mother would say when she returned, but she couldn't think about that now.

After the others went outside, Mandie closed her eyes and tried to get her mind off the pain in her leg. She had just relaxed when she heard someone at the side door.

As Mandie lay there quietly staring up at the ceiling, her own words came back to haunt her. *Why can't you accept. . . ? Why can't you accept. . . ?*

She again saw herself towering over the cradle, telling her little brother she wished he had never been born. *Why can't I accept. . . ?"* she wondered.

She closed her eyes, holding back the tears that threatened to spill down her cheeks. She couldn't let Sallie see her crying. Lifting her thoughts to heaven, she prayed silently, "Please forgive me, dear God, and help me to accept my baby brother."

The next thing Mandie knew, Sallie was shaking her gently. "Mandie, everyone is ready to go now. Do you think you will be all right to travel?"

Mandie slowly pulled herself up. "I hope so," she said. "I can't wait to get home."

Sallie smiled and said, "Oh, I am so happy to hear you say that."

A few minutes later Uncle Ned came into the hospital and carried Mandie out to the wagon. Everybody got in and they returned to Uncle Wirt's house after Uncle Ned hitched the horse he had ridden to Dr. Woodard's buggy so he could bring it along, too.

Uncle Wirt and Aunt Saphronia were concerned about Mandie's injury and insisted she should go to bed immediately after having supper. Mandie pushed herself up on her good leg, hiding the dizziness that momentarily came over her, and said, "Look, I'm fine."

After a lot of arguing Mandie finally convinced everyone she was able to travel all the way home.

It was almost midnight when Uncle Ned and Sallie put their things and Mandie's valise in their wagon and prepared to leave.

"Aren't you coming, Joe?" Mandie asked as Uncle

Ned lifted her into his wagon.

Joe grinned and said, "Well, yes, but I'm driving my father's buggy with the horse your uncle loaned us."

"Don't be too poky," Mandie teased.

Joe grinned again as he went to the waiting buggy.

Mandie smiled at her friends in the yard. "I wish you could all come home with me."

Riley O'Neal patted the side of the wagon. "I'll stay here and look after the hospital until Dr. Woodard gets back," he said. "Then I'll go home to Boston for a while and make plans for the school."

Dimar, standing nearby, asked, "Will you be gone long?"

"Only long enough to finalize the church's plans," the missionary said.

Sallie hugged her grandmother, Morning Star, and handed Mandie her kitten and climbed into the wagon.

"Sallie, I'm so glad you're coming with us," Mandie said, and waving to Morning Star, she called, "I will see you again soon, Morning Star. Love." She blew a kiss to the old woman.

Morning Star grinned and waved.

After everyone said goodbye, Uncle Ned eased the wagon out onto the bumpy country road.

Mandie winced with each jolt. *This isn't going to be an easy trip,* she thought.

The journey was long and slow because Uncle Ned tried to miss all the bumps and holes in the rough dirt road. Mandie was thankful for his kindness, but she wished she could just get home and get it over with.

Joe drove the buggy and stayed right behind them.

They finally arrived at Mandie's house after dinner the

following day. Because the big wagon couldn't go through a lot of shortcuts that pedestrians or horseback riders could, the way was a lot longer than the one Mandie had traveled. But since she had been on foot when she left home that night, it had taken her more time to make the journey.

Uncle Ned pulled the wagon inside the gate and got out to help Mandie into the house. Joe and Sallie followed. Snowball bounced across the yard with them. Joe opened the front door and Uncle Ned took Mandie into the nearby parlor and put her down on the settee.

Elizabeth, who was sitting by the baby's cradle, jumped up. Uncle John was standing at the window and he turned to greet the new arrivals.

"Uncle Ned, what's wrong with Amanda?" Elizabeth exclaimed, hurrying to look at Mandie's bandaged leg. "What happened?" Mandie saw deep love and concern in her mother's eyes.

Elizabeth and John stood there listening intently as Mandie explained. "I'm sorry, Mother," Mandie whispered hoarsely, the tears starting to come again. She pushed back the stray locks of blond hair escaping from her long plait. "I've been so cruel to you and Uncle John. Please forgive me."

Uncle John bent over her to say, "The most important thing for you to realize right now, Amanda, is that your mother and I love you so much. The new baby doesn't change our love for you. We may not be pleased with some of the things you do, but we'll never quit loving you."

Elizabeth knelt beside her daughter and gave her a hug. "Of course, Amanda. We forgive you. I guess we have all been through a lot of adjustments with this new baby. But no matter what, I don't ever want you to doubt our love for you."

Just then the baby woke up, and Mandie could see him in his cradle, kicking and cooing.

"How's my . . . little . . . brother?" She managed to say the words.

Dr. Woodard entered the parlor in time to hear her question. He cleared his throat and sat down by his son near the hearth. "I think that little boy is going to be fine now, Amanda," he said. "I gave him some medicine and he seems much better."

Elizabeth walked over to the cradle and picked up the baby. "Would you like to hold him?" she asked Mandie.

Not quite sure, Mandie sat up and held out her arms hesitantly.

Her mother placed the baby in Mandie's arms, and right away he started howling.

"Stop that crying this minute, Samuel Hezekiah Shaw," she said as she gently swung him back and forth.

The baby instantly hushed and gazed up at Mandie. His big sister smiled down at him in surprise.

Elizabeth looked startled at Mandie's outburst. "I know we said that you could name the baby," she said, "but . . ."

Mandie hurried to explain. "I think we should name him for Aunt Ruby's friend, Samuel Hezekiah Plumbley," she said. She was referring to the Negro doctor who had become a friend of the family.

Uncle John nodded his approval. "That's sweet of you, Amanda. My little sister would appreciate that, I know, if she could have lived to see our baby."

Elizabeth smiled down at them. "We'll have to write to Dr. Plumbley and tell him there are now two Hezekiahs," she said with a laugh.

The baby waved his arms in the air and managed to get his fingers caught in his big sister's hair.

Mandie gently untangled the baby's hand and smiled down at him. *He doesn't look quite as ugly as he did before,* she thought. "I think I'm going to love you, Samuel," she told him.

At that moment Mandie looked up to see her grandmother, Mrs. Taft, coming into the parlor.

"Well, I'm glad you've decided to come home," her grandmother said with a twinkle in her eye. "I was about to cancel our trip to Europe." Then noticing the bandage on Mandie's leg, she asked what happened.

Uncle John took over the explanations and assured Mrs. Taft that Mandie would be fine long before their scheduled sailing date.

Mandie handed little Samuel back to her mother, who returned him to his cradle.

"Then you will let me go with Grandmother to Europe?" Mandie asked. "I was afraid—"

"Yes, Amanda," her mother answered. "I believe you have learned your lesson, and I trust there won't be any more of this running away."

Mandie shook her head silently.

"You have our permission to go, then," Elizabeth said. "Unless something drastic happens to change my mother's plans, you and Celia will be sailing with her next month."

Mandie held her arms up, and Elizabeth bent to give her a hug.

"Oh, Mother," Mandie said, "how could I ever doubt that you love me?"

Elizabeth stood up and wiped a tear from her blue eyes.

Mandie was so glad to be home again. She hurt inside to think of what she had done to her mother by running away. If only there were some way to make up for what she had done . . .

Uncle John put his arm around his wife and looked down at Mandie. "Amanda, I'd say you need a sponge bath and a change of clothes," he said with a little grin. "Then you can come back and make plans with your grandmother for the trip. I'll get Aunt Lou to help you get cleaned up."

Before he got the words out of his mouth, Aunt Lou walked into the room. "My chile!" she exclaimed, looking at the big bandage on Mandie's leg.

Uncle John picked up Mandie and explained what happened as he carried her to the bathroom. Aunt Lou brought in a big chair, and Uncle John set her down on it gently. Then Aunt Lou declared the bathroom off limits to everyone but her and "her chile" until she took care of Mandie.

Even though her leg still throbbed with pain, Mandie felt much better after she got cleaned up, put on fresh clothes, and brushed and braided her hair.

When Uncle John carried her back to the sofa in the parlor, Snowball instantly appeared and jumped up on his mistress's lap. Mandie cuddled the kitten, and he settled down, purring.

Mandie looked up at her grandmother, who sat talking with Elizabeth on the settee across the room. Uncle John joined Dr. Woodard and Joe, who now stood looking out the window.

"Grandmother, could we take Snowball with us to Europe?" Mandie asked.

"Amanda!" her mother shrieked.

"I'm sure Snowball would like to go," Mandie insisted. "And he never gets into any trouble."

Joe laughed out loud. "Oh, is that right?" he asked.

"That's right," Mandie said with a slight pout. "Sometimes he's even smart enough to help when things go wrong. Remember the time he untied the rope when we were kidnapped? And today he led Uncle Ned right to me in the woods."

Joe just shook his head.

Grandmother Taft came over and sat in a chair next to Mandie. "Amanda," she said, patting her granddaughter's hand, "I know how much you love that cat, but I don't see how we could possibly take him on a ship with us. I don't think they would allow it."

"If they do allow it, will you let me take him?" Mandie asked quickly.

"And what would you do with him while we are out sightseeing or dining out, or going to the opera, and all the other things we'll be doing?" her grandmother asked.

"Going to the opera?" Mandie questioned. "Are we? I've never been to an opera."

"I know, dear. That's why we're going." Mrs. Taft patted her faded blond hair into place. "And bless his heart, Senator Morton has promised to escort us."

Just then Mandie caught a glimpse of movement in the hallway. The figure was too small to be Aunt Lou. Then she realized she hadn't seen any of the other servants since they arrived. Where was everyone? she wondered.

Elizabeth also seemed to have seen something in the hall. "Amanda, are you hungry, dear?" she asked.

"I'm starved to death!" Mandie exclaimed.

Joe jumped up. "Come to think of it, other than what your aunt gave us to eat along the way, we haven't had anything to eat since last night," he said. "I'm ready."

Uncle John rose quickly. "Let's all go into the dining room and get something to eat," he suggested, scooping up Mandie into his arms.

They all headed for the dining room, and when Elizabeth slid open the sliding doors, Mandie gasped in astonishment. Inside the dining room, a loud chorus of "Happy Birthday" greeted her. Uncle John stood in the doorway for a moment, then carried her inside.

Mandie couldn't believe her eyes. The room was brightly decorated, and in the center of the long dining room table stood a huge birthday cake decorated in blue.

Uncle John set her down on a chair with a footstool at one end of the table so she could prop up her injured leg. Mandie looked around, trying to take in the whole scene at once.

Everyone was there, it seemed. Standing behind the table at the far side, she saw Uncle Ned, Sallie, Joe, Dr. and Mrs. Woodard, Morning Star, Dimar, Hilda, Polly Cornwallis and her mother, and Mandie's dear friend, Celia Hamilton.

Close by, Aunt Lou came forward in her best white apron and gave Mandie a big hug. "Happy Birthday, my chile!" she cried.

Liza danced around Mandie. "Happy Birthday,

Amanda Shaw," she said. "You is thirteen year old today!"

It hit Mandie by surprise. Today was Thursday, June 6th. Yes, it *was* her birthday, and she had not even remembered. Now she knew why her mother and Uncle John had insisted on her coming home. Mandie's blue eyes filled with tears, and she turned to bury her face in the skirt of Aunt Lou's big white apron.

The old Negro woman used the apron to wipe away the girl's tears. "Now you jes' stop dat cryin', my chile," she said. "It be yo' birthday, and we be havin' a lil' party fo' you."

"Oh, thank you, Aunt Lou. Thank you, everybody," Mandie said in a quavery voice. "This is the first birthday party I ever had."

Everyone surrounded her, and she tried to talk to all of them at once to find out how they all got there.

"It was not easy," Dimar told her. "As soon as you all left, Morning Star and I left in my wagon, and we came as fast as we could." He bent down and whispered, "Morning Star knows some shortcuts, as you call them."

Mandie grinned up at Uncle Ned, and he smiled and nodded, patting her on the back.

"Oh," Dimar added, "your Uncle Wirt and Aunt Saphronia said to tell you they were sorry they could not come. They asked me to tell you happy birthday."

"Your grandmother brought me, of course," Celia said. "My mother and I traveled to her house by train."

Mandie was so happy, she felt as though she were floating on clouds. She was actually thirteen years old today. So many of her friends were there. And she was going to Europe next month.

Elizabeth tapped a goblet lightly with a fork. "Would

everyone please be seated so we can eat supper and then enjoy that beautiful cake?" she said with a little laugh.

As everyone found a place, Uncle Ned smiled down at Mandie. "Papoose come home. Good. Birthday," he said.

Mandie looked up at him and took his old wrinkled hand in hers. "Oh, Uncle Ned, I've been so blessed. I don't deserve all this."

"Papoose make many friends," the old Indian said. "Friends love Papoose. Be thankful."

"I am," Mandie replied simply.

Celia leaned toward her and said, "I'm so sorry you're hurt, but everyone says you should be fine in plenty of time for our trip. Oh, Mandie, we're really going to Europe!" she cried.

"Yes, at last," Mandie said excitedly. "Oh, and something else," she added. "You've just got to go to Birdtown with me when we come back. The Cherokees are going to build a school with help from a church in Boston."

"Boston?" Celia questioned. "That's up north."

"Right, but they're sending money and a man from their church to build a school, and I want to help," Mandie told her friend.

"Then we'll just have to go when we get back from Europe," Celia said.

"With my mother's permission, of course," Mandie added. "And *if* everything works out all right between now and then." Mandie could never be sure.